BEWARE!
DO NOT READ THIS
BOOK FROM
BEGINNING TO END!

Good news: You are about to go on a two-week cruise on the world's most luxurious ship, the S.S. *Finatic*. Even better news: Your parents are staying onshore! You know you and your best friend are sure to have an awesome, parent-free vacation.

That is, until the ship sets sail, and you over-hear another passenger talking about — GULP! A bomb on board! Is this guy just a harmless prankster? Or a real, live terrorist? Will you and your best friend be able to figure it out before your vacation ends with a big BANG?

This scary adventure is all about you. You decide what will happen. And you decide how terrifying the scares will be!

Start on *PAGE 1*. Then follow the instructions at the bottom of each page. You make the choices. If you choose well, you'll make it home again. But if you make the wrong choice . . . BEWARE!

SO TAKE A DEEP BREATH. CROSS YOUR FINGERS. AND TURN TO PAGE 1 NOW TO *GIVE YOURSELF GOOSEBUMPS!*

READER BEWARE —
YOU CHOOSE THE SCARE!

Look for more
GIVE YOURSELF GOOSEBUMPS adventures
from R.L. STINE:

R.L. STINE

GIVE YOURSELF

Goosebumps®

SHIP OF GHOULS

AN
APPLE
PAPERBACK

SCHOLASTIC INC.
New York Toronto London Auckland Sydney
Mexico City New Delhi Hong Kong

A PARACHUTE PRESS BOOK

No part of this publication may be reproduced in whole or in part, or stored in a retrieval system, or transmitted in any form or by any means, electronic, mechanical, photocopying, recording, or otherwise, without written permission of the publisher. For information regarding permission, write to Scholastic Inc., Attention: Permissions Department, 555 Broadway, New York, NY 10012.

ISBN 0-590-51723-6

12 11 10 9 8 7 6 5 4 3 2 1   9/9 0 1 2 3 4/0

Printed in the U.S.A.   40

First Scholastic printing, May 1999

"Awesome!"

"Totally cool!"

"Indeed, quite impressive!"

You, your best friend, Glenn, and your father stand staring at the biggest ocean liner ever built: the SS *Finatic*. Your mom is finishing a call on her cell phone. When she's done, you'll all board the huge cruise ship to Japan.

You can't wait!

"This vessel displaces one hundred thousand tons," your dad declares. "It sails at an average speed of twenty-five knots. Isn't that extraordinary?"

Whatever, you think. It's not like he expects an answer. He's always coming up with "educational" facts and figures.

Your parents are okay. But two weeks alone with them? On a boat? That would be torture!

You're glad Glenn's parents let him take this trip with you. Glenn sometimes acts like a wimp. But he's more fun than *parents*.

You're eager to board. You've seen the brochures. There are video arcades, pools, gyms, a movie theater, awesome food. . . .

BEEP, BEEP, BEEP. Your mom's cell phone interrupts your daydreaming. She answers, then frowns.

"Oh, no!" she groans.

Not a good sign.

Go to PAGE 2.

Your mother clicks her phone off. She slips it into her purse. "There's a work emergency," she explains. Your mom and dad run a business together. "Looks like we have to cancel the trip."

"What?" you cry. "You can't do that! We're about to board."

You're about to start whining and moaning. But it's not like you're four years old. You're twelve.

Try logic, you think.

"Glenn and I can still make the trip," you argue. "We'll be okay. I mean, we'll be on a boat. A contained environment. What could go wrong?"

Your parents give you a look. Then they talk quietly with each other. Finally they chat with the ship's steward.

"I'll keep an eye on them," the steward promises.

Which makes you want to laugh. Because the steward has weird, bulging eyes that never seem to blink. But you control yourself.

Your mom phones Glenn's folks. They agree to let him go.

"Yes!" You and Glenn slap high fives.

In two weeks your parents will fly to Japan and meet you when the ship docks. Until then you and Glenn are totally parent-free!

Let the fun begin!

It starts on PAGE 9.

You have to get away from these maniacs!

You shove Fisher into the crewmen. Hard! They fall down in a heap.

"Let's book!" you yell to Glenn. You both start running at top speed.

You race up the steps. You hear Fisher and the crew right behind you. You push open the door leading to the main deck.

Fisher's voice echoes in the stairwell. "Those kids will wish they'd never been born," he shouts.

YIKES!

You exit the stairway on a floor with a sign that says MAIN DECK.

Whoa! The main deck is the length of three football fields. The stairs let you out midship. In front of you, you see rows of cabin doors. Behind you the enormous lounge is filled with passengers.

Which way should you go to flee from the crew?

Run forward on PAGE 16.

Or turn around and head for the crowded lounge on PAGE 7.

What you see is terrifying. The bottom half of the creature is a man. The top half is pure shark. Fins instead of arms. A mouth lined with teeth like chain saws. The hairs on the back of your neck stand up.

Glenn freaks. "Can we go back on deck? *Now?*"

You shake your head. There's only one real way out of this whole thing, you realize.

You turn to Bosco. "How can we find The Room?"

"*Now* you want me to help you?" he answers sharply.

"Please!" you beg. Begging is a whole lot better than dying.

Bosco sighs. He pokes his head back out of the shell. "Go through that cage door. The Room is back there."

"I don't trust Bosco," Glenn whispers. "He may want to get back at us. We should go that way." He points to a door at the end of a catwalk — ten feet above the floor.

The only way you can reach that door is by climbing a rope dangling from the catwalk's steel framework. Not so easy.

But the shark-man stands between you and the cage door. Even less easy.

To try to make it past the shark, go to PAGE 80.
To climb up to the catwalk, go to PAGE 62.

There are about twenty prisoners in the cage —
all passengers from the ship. They're dressed in
swimsuits and shorts. Some have white sunscreen
on their noses. Most are sitting or lying on the
cold floor. They look sick.

"I feel nauseous!" a woman moans.

"Please, help me!" another cries.

The door of the cage has an electronic lock with
numbers on it. To open it, you need to punch in the
correct code. A green light indicates the door is already open.

"They must be too weak to leave the cage," you
realize. "We need to help them out."

You and Glenn step inside.

Suddenly the door clangs shut behind you. The
sound makes you jump.

"Hey!" You wheel around. The person who shut
the door has already darted around the corner.

You glance at the lock. The light on it glows red.
You know what that means.

You yank on the door.

Yup. It's locked!

Go to PAGE 50.

You have to warn security about Bosco's threat. If he does have a bomb and you don't report him . . . well, that would make you —

Dead?

You find a crewman on the upper deck. You and Glenn tell him everything. Well, *you* do. Glenn just snickers. But the crewman takes it very seriously. He runs off to tell the captain.

A few minutes later you see some big, hulking guys tearing through the door to the lower deck.

"Let's follow them," you whisper to Glenn.

He nods. "I want to see what happens to that nutcase."

You peek around the side of a wall. You spot the crewmen shoving Bosco into a room. They slam the door shut. Then one of them pulls something out of Bosco's bag.

Your eyes widen in astonishment. You can't believe it.

It's a bomb! Bosco was telling the truth.

But why does he want to blow up the ship? you wonder.

And, you can't help but think, was he telling the truth about the other stuff too? Are you in danger?

Turn to PAGE 21.

You'll be safe around people, you decide. So you dart into the huge, fancy lounge. You and Glenn try to blend in with the passengers.

You notice Fisher nearby. He nods to his men. They begin working their way toward you through the crowd. You break into a sweat.

"What are we going to do?" Glenn asks fearfully.

You spot some passengers huddled around the cruise director.

"Okay, we have lots of fun activities," he announces. "Who wants to sign up for mini-golf? I also have openings for our darts tournament. And I'm looking for a volunteer to be the magician's assistant in tonight's show."

"We'll be okay as long as we hang with the passengers," you tell Glenn. "We should sign up for something."

Which activity should you pick?
If you choose mini-golf, go to PAGE 23.
If you choose darts, go to PAGE 17.
If you choose the magic show, go to PAGE 19.

"The passengers are going to be turned into monsters," Bosco declares.

WHAT?

"You have to be kidding." Glenn rolls his eyes.

"This is no joke," Bosco shouts. "The same scientist ran a cruise last year. I was the only one to survive. The others were all changed into hideous *things*. In a place called The Room. I never found out the scientist's name. But I've been tracking the cruise lines. This is *his* handiwork. I must stop the horror from happening again!"

"What are people being changed into?" Glenn asks.

Before he can answer, you hear the crew returning!

"Quick," you tell Glenn. "We have to get out of here."

You duck around a corner. You watch two burly crewmen open the door. They drag Bosco out.

"We're taking you to The Room," one growls.

"No!" Bosco screeches. "Noooo!"

The Room — the one Bosco was talking about — exists, you realize. Does that mean the rest of his story is true?

And an even bigger question: What should you do now? Go after them? Or get some help?

If you go after Bosco yourself, go to PAGE 33.
If you find help, go to PAGE 22.

A crew member leads you and Glenn to your cabin on B Deck.

It's tiny — but totally cool! You peer out a round window — the porthole. You're high above the waterline.

"There's a map of the ship on the desk," the sailor tells you.

"Thanks." You glance at him.

Strange, you think as you watch him leave. How can he stay so pale working on a cruise ship? He almost looks . . . slimy.

You find a souvenir magnet in the shape of the *Finatic*. You slip it into your pocket. Right next to a paper clip, some gum, and some other junk.

You glance at your watch. The ship is about to leave. You're excited. But you're also a little nervous being on your own.

Not that you would *ever* admit that to Glenn!

"Let's check out this ship!" you declare.

"Deal." Glenn grins. He grabs the map. Then you head out to explore.

"Okay, where should we go first?" Glenn unfolds the map and studies it. "Arcade? Pool?"

It *all* sounds fun. "Let's just wander around," you suggest.

Up ahead several crew members huddle together. They stop talking as you and Glenn pass.

That's weird, you think. What's the big secret?

Stroll to PAGE 48.

Gross! It's a rat!

Get used to it.

Day after day you and Glenn sit on the cold floor. Day after day you wait for food and water.

But nothing arrives. You don't know which is worse — being thirsty or being hungry. Either way, you feel weaker and weaker.

"They don't treat you like this on the *Love Boat*," you complain to Glenn. "My parents are going to ask for their money back."

Glenn doesn't respond. He just sits in a corner of the room, crying.

Without food and water, you eventually become so weak you just fall asleep. When the ship lands in Japan, your parents never hear your complaints about the service. Because by then, your vacation — and you — have come to an early

END.

The whale shoots out a spume of water.

"Let's get out of here!" you order. You and Judy don't stop paddling until the whale is a dot in the distance.

Steve sighs. "We're still out of food."

Maybe not. You notice two seabirds flying near the boat. They're fighting over a fish in one bird's beak. As you watch, the bird drops the fish. It falls into the ocean, a few feet from the boat.

Before either bird can dive for it, you grab an oar. You use it to scoop the fish out of the water.

"Food!" you cry. You bring the oar carefully back into the boat. "We have food!" You hold up the fish proudly.

Then it hits you: You have to eat it raw! Yuck!

But you have no choice. You all take bites. Not bad, you think. No worse than cafeteria mystery meat.

Bob is about to polish off the fish when Steve stops him. "Let's use some of the flesh as bait to catch more fish."

Bob shakes his head. "We need all the nourishment we can get. I say eat it to the bone."

They look at you. "What should we do?" Judy asks you.

If you decide to finish the fish, go to PAGE 97.
If you decide to use some as bait, go to PAGE 57.

You learn that the captain is in the navigation room on the top deck. You knock on the door.

"Come in," a voice booms. You stick your head in. The captain beckons you to approach. He's a tall, silver-haired man with a beard. "How can I help you?"

You tell him your story. He springs into action. "Mr. Fisher," he barks at his lieutenant. "Go with these children. Question the man with the bomb. If someone is using this cruise to harm our passengers, I want to know about it!"

"Aye, sir!" Fisher replies.

You lead Fisher to the room where you last saw Bosco.

Hey! The room is empty. A couple of crewmen huddle nearby.

Fisher wheels around, facing you and Glenn.

"We can't let you interfere with our plans," he snarls. "But we'll get rid of you before you spook the passengers. We offered this cheap cruise as bait. And all you suckers fell for it."

"You don't scare me," you declare. "The captain —"

Fisher interrupts you. "Take them to The Room!" he thunders.

Okay. That's it. He just officially scared you.

Go to PAGE 3.

"Ohhhhh!" you groan. You're seasick.

You feel like puking.

And you do. Right over the side of the lifeboat.

Everyone is totally grossed out. So you sit alone, feeling sorry for yourself. You wish you never went on that stupid cruise.

You huddle against the side of the boat with your eyes shut, groaning softly.

Toward evening you feel a little better. When the sun drops below the horizon, you fall into a deep sleep.

Turn to PAGE 25.

Uh-oh! What did you get yourself into? This man is nuts! What if he attacks you?

You and Glenn take a few steps backwards. "Sorry we bothered you, Mr. —"

"Bosco," the man mutters. "My name is Tom Bosco. And one day the world will thank me." He rummages in his bag.

You can tell Glenn is as weirded-out as you are. "Easy, Mr. Bosco." You try to sound soothing. Calm. You point to the bag. "What's in there?"

"It's a bomb!" Bosco declares. "I'm going to blow up the ship."

You stare at him, stunned. Without warning he pushes past you and out to the stairwell. You hear him clattering down the steps.

Glenn bursts out laughing. "What a weirdo!"

But what if Bosco was telling the truth? you wonder. "Maybe we should tell the crew about him," you suggest.

"Nah," Glenn declares. "We'd freak people out for nothing. If they even believe us."

If you tell the ship's security about Bosco, go to PAGE 6.

If you ignore the nut, go to PAGE 75.

Then the plane swings around.

It's returning! As it passes over the boat, it dips its wings. The pilot is letting you know he spotted the boat.

You all cheer. "We're saved!" you shout. Even Bob is grinning.

Ten hours later a coast guard boat picks you up. They radio to your parents that you're safe. Very soon you arrive in California.

You've never been so glad to see your parents in all your life.

"You must be starved!" Your mom squeezes you close. She asks someone for directions to the closest nice restaurant.

In a few minutes you're seated in a fancy sushi restaurant.

Sushi? you think. Sounds good.

You stare down at a plate of raw fish.

Aw, man! Too bad sushi didn't mean a big fat cheeseburger for you in —

THE END.

"This way!" You dash forward. You and Glenn try every cabin door lining the corridor. But they're all locked!

Your feet pound as you tear along the corridor. "This is like running a marathon," you huff to Glenn.

You burst through a set of double doors at the end of the hall.

You're at the front of the ship. You gaze at the deep blue ocean.

"You've reached the end of the line," a voice says.

You whirl around. Fisher smiles a nasty smile. He snaps his fingers. He and his crew advance toward you and Glenn.

You slowly back up. Until you bump into the deck rail. Behind you is nothing but open sea.

You're feeling desperate. So you come up with a desperate plan.

You put one leg over the rail. "Come any closer and we'll jump," you yell.

"We will?" Glenn squeaks.

The crew pulls up short. For a moment. Then they keep coming.

Plan A isn't working. So you come up with Plan B.

"Jump!" you scream to Glenn.

And you leap over the rail.

Land on PAGE 34.

Glenn opts for mini-golf. But you're pretty good at darts.

You and Glenn decide to split up. You figure it will make you less conspicuous if you're not trying to hide as a pair. So you head inside for the game room alone. There are billiard tables and chess and backgammon boards. Professional dartboards hang on the wall. The tournament director hands you a bunch of brass darts.

"You go first," she orders.

You hold the dart between your thumb and forefinger. You aim at the dartboard and let fly.

Bull's-eye!

"Yes!" you cheer. You hear applause from the crowd.

You throw the rest of your darts. You collect a super score. This is so much fun, you've forgotten the jam you're in.

You walk up to the board. You pull out your darts.

And scream in pain.

Go to PAGE 130.

The tiger opens its very large mouth.

And you see its very large teeth.

Maybe it's tame! After all, it does tricks.

"N-nice kitty," you stammer.

Only your words aren't very clear. Because your teeth are chattering.

The giant cat pounces. You try to get away. But it outweighs you by about three hundred fifty pounds. There's not much you can do. . . .

On the bright side, you figure out the secret to Zelmo's disappearing trick.

Zelmo is going to make you disappear, all right.

Inside the tiger's stomach!

THE END

Being a magician's assistant sounds like fun. You and Glenn volunteer to help Zelmo the Magnifico.

Zelmo has stringy black hair and wears an old black cape. He leads you and Glenn to the ship's theater. It's empty at this time of day. This makes you nervous. You were hoping for safety in numbers.

Zelmo locks the door. "I don't vant anyone to figure out my zecrets," he declares in a weird accent.

Well, you think, at least no one can get in. Glenn sits facing the stage. He's your only audience.

Zelmo pulls you onstage. "Vee vill rehearse our parts for tonight," he tells you. He points to a box. "You go in zis," Zelmo explains. "I put tiger inside. Then raise box in air. I bring box down. You no longer in box."

Hey, that sounds cool.

Rehearse on PAGE 31.

"Please let there be an unlocked door," you murmur.

You and Glenn race down the carpeted corridor. You turn the knob on every door. They're all locked.

You know that guy Fisher will turn up any second. You try to fight your panic. You rush down another corridor.

Yes! Luck is finally on your side. An unlocked door! You peek into the cabin. It's empty!

You and Glenn dart inside. You flip the lock.

"Check it out." Glenn holds up an envelope. The name FISHER is scrawled across it.

"What's up with that?" you ask Glenn. He hands it to you.

You open the envelope. You pull out a sheet of plastic-coated paper with this formula on it: $TS = 2M \times 1/2P + 1/8S + 1/16P$.

Huh?

You were always lousy at math. So you're not surprised the formula makes no sense to you. "Maybe it has something to do with the experiments on board the ship," Glenn suggests.

Could be. So you stuff the paper into your pocket.

Uh-oh. Voices outside the door! The knob jiggles. Then it turns.

You're about to be busted!

Go to PAGE 86.

You have to talk to Tom Bosco and find out the truth.

You and Glenn hide as the crew leaves. Then you creep to the door at the end of the corridor. You yank on the knob.

But the door is locked. Duh! Big surprise.

You glance over your shoulder. Good. No sign of the crew. You knock on the door.

"What do you want?" a voice inside asks.

"We're the guys who turned you in," Glenn explains.

"Real smart, Glenn," you groan.

Bosco goes bonkers. "You idiots!" he shouts through the door. "You'll soon wish I destroyed this ship. And everyone on it."

You hate being called an idiot. But you stifle your anger. "What's the deal?" you ask. "Tell us and maybe we can help."

"The deal is this." Bosco's voice drips with cold fury. "This whole cruise is phony. It was set up by a lunatic. A mad person who intends to use the passengers as guinea pigs in a horrible experiment."

You gasp. "What kind of experiment?"

Now Bosco's voice quavers with fear. "To turn passengers into . . . into . . ."

Into what?

Find out on PAGE 8.

You can't go after Bosco on your own. You need help. But who can you ask? Who will believe your unbelievable story?

You and Glenn sneak back up to the main deck. You pass through a tremendous lounge. Passengers sit and sip iced tea, read, and relax.

If they knew what was really going on with this cruise they wouldn't look so calm, you think. You run your hand nervously through your hair. You wonder what to do.

Someone taps you on the shoulder. You turn and see a woman with salt-and-pepper hair and a fancy, flowered scarf around her neck.

"My name is Mrs. Bass. You look upset. Can I help you?" She seems like a nice lady. So you tell her about Bosco.

Mrs. Bass looks shocked. "If this man is telling the truth, we're in danger. The authorities must be alerted."

Another passenger overhears your conversation. He bursts out laughing. "My name's Smith. I think you should ignore Bosco's story. He sounds like a loon." He rubs his stubbly chin.

Mrs. Bass disagrees. "Tell the captain. He'll help."

Smith seems kind of obnoxious. He gives you bad vibes. You decide to take Mrs. Bass's advice. You go search for the captain.

Search for him on PAGE 12.

You follow a group to the recreation deck. The area is so big, it holds a nine-hole mini-golf course *and* two swimming pools. This would be a blast — if Fisher weren't threatening to kill you.

You pick up a club and place your golf ball down on the first tee. This is a simple L-shaped hole. You line up the putt and bank the ball off the wood sideboard. Hole in one!

The next hole is decorated with a four-foot-tall red barn. You knock the ball through two small open doors.

Bingo! Another hole in one. Then you face a windmill with moving blades. You time it just right. The ball plops right into the hole.

You hit nine holes in one. Then you repeat the course. You ace it again. The crowd cheers wildly. Even Fisher applauds!

The cruise director rushes over. "You're the greatest player ever," he gushes. "I want to make you our mini-golf pro."

You accept. Not only is the cruise free, but you get paid for playing!

Fisher tries to convince you to make him your manager. He figures there's more money in mini-golf than in evil experiments. Instead, you decide to make him your caddy.

But the best part is, you love your new life. Becoming a mini-golf pro fits you to a tee!

THE END

You let Glenn talk you into eating first.

Wow! The snack bar is like a dream come true. It's filled with dessert stations, sandwich bars, pasta salads, and fruit baskets.

"I can't wait to see the spread for dinner," you exclaim.

Best of all — the food is free. And you can get seconds! Thirds even.

The only bummer is the people serving the food. They're not very friendly. They act as if they resent you being there. Some of the servers snicker at the passengers when they think no one's looking — as if they know a funny secret.

Whatever. You're not going to let them spoil your fun.

You scarf down a burger and stuff a ham sandwich into your pocket.

Now it's time to follow that suspicious-looking dude.

On to PAGE 54!

You wake up before dawn. You're incredibly thirsty. You crawl over to the water container. You lift it to your lips.

"What are you doing?" Bob yells. Everyone is jolted awake.

"We don't know when we're going to be rescued," he screams. "Each person can only drink a half cup of water a day. From now on, don't touch the water without my permission. Or else!"

"Chill," Steve tells Bob. "You're getting on everyone's last nerve."

You fume at the other end of the boat. Far away from Bob.

The sun beats down every day. Everyone worries about being rescued — before the food and water run out.

After ten days on the lifeboat, you haven't spotted a ship or a plane. There's only enough water for a few more days.

That night you have trouble sleeping. You open your eyes and discover a thick fog surrounding the lifeboat. It's hard to see.

Your senses go on alert. You hear a scraping noise. You spot a white shape moving silently at the other end of the boat. It's a swirly, ghostly figure.

"Who's there?" you whisper.

Instead of an answer, you hear a bloodcurdling cry. Then a loud splash.

Find out what's going on on PAGE 108.

"Where's Judy?" Steve cries.

It's not as if there is anywhere to hide on a lifeboat. And you don't see her in the water, either. What happened to her?

You clear your throat. "I saw something last night," you admit. "It looked like a ghost. I saw it once before but I didn't say anything. I-I was afraid you would laugh at me."

Bob rolls his eyes. "You were dreaming."

"No!" Steve exclaims. "I saw the same thing. And I saw it when it disappeared too!" He folds his arms across his chest. "I think this boat is haunted by a ghost from the *Finatic*! And he's getting rid of us one by one!"

"Oh, give me a break," Bob sneers.

Trapped on a boat with a killer ghost? You know it's a crazy idea. Then you have a terrible thought: Could the ghost want revenge because you didn't alert the crew about the mad bomber?

You shudder. Then a strange sound interrupts your thoughts.

Now what? Find out on PAGE 99.

You swim to the island on your left. It's hard-going, but you make it. Powerful waves carry you up and onto the beach.

You stumble a few feet away from the surf. Then you collapse on the sand, totally wiped out. Within seconds you fall asleep.

When you wake up, it's late afternoon. You figure you might as well explore the beach. But you don't find much.

No sign of Steve, Bob, or anyone else. You have the feeling you won't find any tourists, souvenir stands, or hotels, either.

At the edge of the beach rises a thick forest. Maybe you'll find Bob and Steve in there. You enter the forest.

Tropical flowers grow everywhere. Colorful birds flit from branch to branch. It's a beautiful scene.

But you don't enjoy it. You're alone and lost. Hopelessness washes through you.

You walk for hours. As evening comes, exhaustion and fear overtake you. You tear off large leaves from a tree and lay them on the ground. That's your bed.

You lie down under the stars, wondering if you'll survive.

Go to PAGE 101.

The tiger is an inch from you. You feel its hot breath on your cheek. Then you get a hot idea.

Slowly — *verrrrrry* slowly — you reach into your pocket. You pull out the ham sandwich you saved from lunch earlier and offer it to the tiger.

It gulps down the sandwich. You hope it likes mustard.

Then the tiger licks your face with its rough tongue.

Whew! You breathe a sigh of relief.

While you and the big cat bond, the box is lowered.

Zelmo opens the front flap of the box. He jumps back, astonished you are alive.

You scuttle out and brush by Zelmo.

"Come on, Glenn!" you shout. You both race out of the theater and onto the main deck. It won't take long for Zelmo to alert the crew that you've gotten away. They'll be looking for you.

So where do you hide?

You spot a corridor lined with cabins. If you're lucky, you'll find an open one.

Head for the cabins on PAGE 20.

Everyone buzzes with excitement. You and Judy grab the oars. You paddle hard toward the gray island.

But when you get closer, you discover it's not an island after all. . . .

It's a whale.

"But, hey," Steve exclaims. "A whale is food. And we could definitely use some."

"How can we kill it?" Judy asks.

You have an idea. "With the flare gun!"

"No," Bob declares. "That's dangerous. We should get out of here. If you shoot and miss, it could become angry and tip us over."

If you use the flare, go to PAGE 93.
If you paddle away, go to PAGE 11.

Then you remember. The flare gun!

You fling open the locker and grab the flare gun. You point it to the sky and fire.

BLAM!

The smoky flare shimmers high in the air. Then it explodes in a bright orange light. It hangs for a moment before sinking slowly.

You hold your breath. The pilot must have seen *that*!

The plane keeps flying away.

"No!" Bob moans.

You slump to the bottom of the boat. That's it, you think. I give up.

We're goners!

Turn to PAGE 15.

You climb into the box. Zelmo closes it.

"Now I put tiger in," he explains. "Ven I open box, audience see tiger. But you have disappeared. Good trick, yes?"

"Aren't you going to teach me how to do it first?"

Zelmo doesn't answer. Instead, he opens up the back of the box. A huge tiger steps in. Zelmo slams the box shut fast.

The tiger growls. You scrunch against the far end of the box. But the far end isn't much farther than the near end.

"Help!" you scream. "Let me out!"

The tiger growls again.

"Hi, guy," you whisper to the tiger. "Let's be friends."

You feel the box being lifted in the air.

The tiger licks its chops. With a hungry gaze it pads toward you. You can smell its foul tiger breath.

You know it wants to eat something — but it better not be you!

Did you stop earlier for a snack? Then go to PAGE 28.

If you didn't eat, go to PAGE 18.

You figure Smith is the Boss. He tried to keep you from going to the captain. And Mrs. Bass is so kind and helpful.

"Take that!" You empty the fire extinguisher on Smith. He howls in pain as the chemicals seep into his eyes. While he's helpless, you reach for the needle. Smith swings the syringe blindly, just missing you. Glenn tackles him to the floor. You sit on Smith's chest and grab the needle.

"No, you've made a mistake," he groans.

"Yeah, sure," you retort. "Like when you said Bosco wasn't telling the truth."

While Smith is down, you and Glenn roll him over. You tie his hands together with some electrical cord.

You turn around to make sure Mrs. Bass is okay. But she has a funny way of thanking you for saving her.

She jabs Glenn with her syringe, injecting him with fish DNA!

Go to PAGE 83.

"Come on, Glenn," you whisper. "Let's give Bosco a hand."

"Uh, I don't know," he replies.

Typical Glenn, you think. Wimping out. But you got poor Bosco into this mess. You want to try to get him out of it.

You dash into the corridor. And into a group of crew members. Including the steward who promised your folks he'd look after you.

You're not sure what comes over you, but you feel as if you have to say, "You better leave that guy Bosco alone, or — or —"

Or what? Your mind goes blank.

"These kids saw too much. Seize them," the steward commands.

Before you can escape, four crew members grab you and Glenn. They shove you into a dark cabin. Without furniture or lights.

You pound on the door with your fists. "When my parents find out about this, you'll all be in big trouble!"

"I think they're gone," Glenn tells you.

You shudder. The dark walls seem to be closing in on you.

And as if things weren't already creepy enough, you hear a skittering noise on the floor in front of you.

Go to PAGE 10.

SPLASH!

Did you and Glenn fall into the ocean? You tread water and glance around.

No! You landed in a swimming pool!

"We need to get out of sight," you tell Glenn. You scramble out of the pool.

Nearby are the crew's sleeping quarters. You sneak inside. Luckily, it's empty. You and Glenn duck behind a large trunk.

Two crewmen enter. "We'll get those pesky kids," one mutters. "They can't hide forever on a ship."

You peer around the side of the trunk. You watch a crewman grab a shaker full of fish food. That's weird, you think. I don't see a fish tank anywhere.

He holds the shaker up and sprinkles it — *into his mouth!*

Gross!

When the other crewman takes off his shirt, you see something even grosser.

Eeeew! Go to PAGE 98.

Glenn squeezes through the porthole. Then it's your turn.

Oh, no! You're stuck! Behind you, you hear the bathroom door splinter open.

"It's those kids!" Fisher yanks at your feet.

Glenn pulls on your arms. A tug-of-war is going on, and *you're* the rope.

"Pull harder!" you scream at Glenn. He jerks with such force that you pop out of the porthole and flop onto the deck.

You scramble to your feet and race past joggers on the sun-soaked deck. You glance back. An angry Fisher is right behind you.

"Why don't you just give him the formula?" Glenn moans.

"No way. I want to know why it's so valuable," you answer.

You try to lose Fisher by making a quick left. Now you're at the entrance to the main dining hall. You dart inside the empty room. But Fisher is still on your tail. Unbelievable!

There's one last place to flee: the kitchen. You push through the swinging doors. Inside, cooks are preparing dinner. One is pouring milk into a big mixing machine. She's making ice cream.

You have to get rid of the formula before Fisher catches you.

You drop the plastic sheet into the ice cream maker. The formula disappears.

Reappear on PAGE 66.

"The formula must be in the cake!" you whisper to Glenn.

You and Glenn rush over to the cake. You smoosh it with your hands. Ice cream splatters everywhere. Frosting drips between Glenn's fingers.

Diners yell at you to stop. But you don't. Because you're sure this cake has more in it than calories.

"I've got it!" Glenn holds up the formula. But the chef snatches it out of Glenn's cake-covered hands.

"You found this in my cake?" Henri demands. "What is it?" He reads the formula and frowns. Then his face brightens. "Ah! It is a recipe. For tartar sauce."

Tartar sauce? Fisher wanted to start an operation to produce tartar sauce?

You're totally confused.

Turn to PAGE 81.

You and Glenn head for the garbage bags. You open one up and hop in.

YEECH!

It's full of leftover food.

It stinks. But after several hours, you get used to the smell. You even nibble on a half-eaten cream puff.

Glenn chews a slice of corn bread. "Not bad," he decides.

After a short while, someone picks up the bag.

"Man, this is heavy," an annoyed voice gasps.

The bag is dragged down some stairs.

THUMP! THUMP! THUMP! THUMP!

Ouch! Ouch! Ouch! Ouch!

You're bruised all over. Maybe we should have bagged this idea, you think.

The bag is dropped on a cement floor. After a few minutes of silence, you whisper to Glenn, "We should get out of here. Before they dump us into the incinerator or something."

Climb out of your stinky hiding place on PAGE 94.

You glance around the pantry. Bingo!

"Get into the vat of worms," you order Glenn.

"You've got to be kidding!" he retorts.

"Look," you explain. "This vat is marked for D Deck. If we hide inside it they'll take us there. I know it."

Glenn gives in. He slips into a vat full of live, wriggling worms. You join him.

Ugh! The glistening worms crawl all over you. You keep your mouth shut tight so they can't crawl in. The red wriggling creatures are in your hair, sliding into your ears.

Gross! This is the most disgusting thing you've ever done. It's off the Barf-o-Meter.

You wait an hour. Trying not to breathe in the earthworms.

Then the vat starts moving.

You feel it rumble. You, Glenn, and the worms bounce around, then stop.

You wait until it seems safe. Then you climb out of the vat, covered in slime.

Yes! You made it to D Deck!

Go to PAGE 42.

From a countertop you grab a syringe filled with fluid.

It's a duel to the death!

"Get ready to rumble!" you shout at Mrs. Bass.

You slowly circle each other. She thrusts forward. Her weapon just misses you.

That was close! If you get stuck, you're out of luck. *Focus!* you order yourself.

You strike at her — and miss. She counterattacks. With a cry of triumph, she stabs you in the arm.

You gaze down in horror. And see that the needle missed your skin. Instead it sliced clean through your sleeve and buried itself in some corkboard on the wall.

As Mrs. Bass tries to pull out the needle, you strike. Your syringe jabs into her arm. You inject fish DNA into her.

She doubles over in pain. While she's out of it, you check on Glenn. He's stretched out, shaking and sweating.

"Are you okay?" you ask him.

Of course he's not okay! He's turning into a sea horse! You feel awful. You don't know what to do to help him!

Then you feel an awful stinging sensation.

Get the point on PAGE 88.

"We'll never fit through the porthole," you whisper to Glenn. "We better go down the chute."

Glenn slides down feet first. Now it's your turn. You're just about through when the bathroom door bursts open.

Fisher spots you. "It's that kid!" he screams.

"Later, Fisher!" You wave as you disappear down the chute.

The narrow metal tunnel is like a water-flume ride — without the water.

"OOOF!" You crash right on top of Glenn.

You both land on a large pile of dirty towels. You glance around. You're in the ship's laundry room. It's filled with huge washing and drying machines. Steam shoots out of pressers. Large hampers on wheels are filled with dirty sheets.

You jump up. "Pretend everything's totally normal," you coach Glenn. You stroll past the cleaning crew, toward the exit. But before you reach it, you see Fisher skidding to a halt at the doorway.

Go to PAGE 47.

You enter a honeycomb of storage areas. You realize everything needed during the voyage is kept in here. You find plenty of mops, ropes, tools, machinery — but nothing that looks like it could be The Room. Nothing even suspicious.

Dejected, you walk down still another corridor. You hear voices coming your way.

"Quick," you whisper to Glenn. "In here." You duck into the ship's vast pantry. Boxes of bread and cereals and plastic containers of beverages are piled high.

But you notice something bizarre.

You spot several barrels of chum — mashed-up seafood used as fish bait. There also are vats filled with live worms. As well as big tubs of fish food flakes. Why do they need these on a cruise?

You peer closely and see that all the containers of fish food are stenciled FOR D DECK.

"I don't remember seeing D Deck on the map," Glenn says.

"That's weird," you respond. "And why do they need worms and chum down there?"

You find the door to D Deck. But it's locked.

"Well, we found the way to the mystery deck," you declare. "Now the mystery is how to get inside."

Go to PAGE 38.

D Deck is dark and dank. Water drips from overhead pipes. The air is clammy. You creep along, your heart pounding. You have no idea what you're going to find down here.

You reach a dead end. There's a single iron hatch in the floor.

"Well, there's nowhere to go but down," you declare.

"That's what I was afraid of," Glenn mumbles.

You turn a wheel to open the hatch. You stare down into blackness. A ladder descends into . . . what?

"Did I ever tell you I'm afraid of the dark?" Glenn asks.

"What aren't you afraid of?" you respond with a sigh.

"I'm not afraid of worms anymore," he answers.

As you climb down, you step into water. The place is flooded! By the time you touch the floor of the chamber, the water is up to your waist.

You glance around the chamber. In the dim light you notice only one other way out — a hatch on the opposite wall. You and Glenn slosh forward.

Something touches the back of your leg. A chill runs through you.

Because Glenn is in front of you.

Go to PAGE 124.

None of the tribesmen follows you across the crocodile heads. Instead, they race around the edge of the lake. If they catch you . . . well, forget about it.

You dash into the woods, thrashing through thick vegetation.

You find a dirt path. After a short while, the path divides. One branch goes up a steep hill. It's narrow and twisting. If you follow it, the tribesmen won't be able to see you. Of course, you have no idea where it leads.

The other branch leads left, down to the beach. That's where Bob said he saw a canoe. Trouble is, this branch is wide and straight. You'll be easy to spot.

You hear the cries of angry tribesmen behind you.

You have to make a decision — fast.

If you run up the hill, go to PAGE 112.
If you sprint toward the sea, go to PAGE 119.

"Let's try to short out the lock," you decide.

Glenn agrees. "Cool." He stoops to pick up the eel.

"Wait!" you shout. "Electric eels produce major voltage. If you touch it, you'll fry."

You glance around the cage. That's it!

You're both wearing running shoes with rubber soles. Rubber doesn't conduct electricity.

You take off your shoes and stick your hands into them. Using the sneakers as mittens, you and Glenn pick up the eel.

You carry the eel to the door and slap it against the electric lock. There's a crackling noise. The lock short-circuits and the light turns green. The steel door is now unlocked.

You fling it open.

But the fish-people are right behind you!

Flee to PAGE 68.

A hunk of metal whizzes by your head. Smoke pours across the deck. Your heart pounds in terror. Is the boat going to sink?

With a tremendous grinding noise, the ship splits in two. You and Glenn are thrown to the deck. People dart in all directions, screaming in panic.

Glenn's face pales. His eyes are wide with horror.

"Don't freak out," you order him. You try to stay calm. Then you check out the crew. Their faces are twisted in fear.

That's it. You lose it.

"It's all our fault!" you wail. "We should have warned someone about the bomb!"

"We can't worry about that now," Glenn cries. "What do we do?"

A man runs past you. "Where are the lifeboats?" he yells.

The lifeboats! Yes! You might live after all!

"We have to find those lifeboats," you tell Glenn.

But before you can move, the ship's bow lurches into the water. You and Glenn slide backwards along the deck. You grab the handrails. Glenn hangs on to you.

The water rushes at you. With a burbling sound the ship slides into the ocean. Taking everyone with it. Including you and Glenn!

Go to PAGE 70.

You try to sprint through the waist-high water to the hatch. But you can't move very quickly. The water is holding you back!

You stop for a second to glance back.

No lobsters! They must have gone underwater.

You churn through the water, running for your life. Your heart is ready to burst. From effort. From terror.

Suddenly there's a loud splash next to you!

Go to PAGE 58.

You grab the clothes hamper. "Get in," you urge Glenn.

You and Glenn climb in. You dive under the dirty towels.

A moment later the hamper starts rolling.

You hear Fisher call, "Wait. Stop that hamper!"

The hamper stops moving. Your heart begins to pound hard.

You feel Fisher pull aside some towels from the top of your pile. You're almost exposed! He can nearly see you! You hold your breath and shut your eyes.

"Forget it," Fisher mutters impatiently. "They're not in there. I've got to find them and get that paper back."

The hamper starts moving. You breathe again. You made it!

Suddenly one side of the hamper tilts down. You and Glenn are flung out into an industrial-size washing machine.

"Let us out!" you holler. But no one can hear you.

Uh-oh. You're really in hot water now. In fact, by the end of the spin cycle, you're all washed up.

THE END

You and Glenn turn a corner. Then you climb up a flight of stairs. Then you turn another corner.

And come face-to-face with a huge silver door. You reach for the door handle.

"Stop right there," a voice booms behind you. You and Glenn slowly turn around.

A sailor in a *Finatic* uniform strides toward you. He plasters a big smile on his face. "Sorry, kids. Equipment room. Off-limits."

On your way back to the main corridor Glenn studies the map.

"Weird," Glenn mutters. "That door isn't on the map."

"Really?" You peer at the map. He's right.

"We should double-check where we are," you suggest. "We might be reading this map wrong. Let's go ask that sailor."

You head back around the corner. The sailor is gone.

But you notice a passenger carrying a black bag. He's a plump, older guy with a round face and a bad haircut. He glances around. Then bolts through the silver door.

What's his story? "Glenn, let's follow that guy," you suggest.

"Nah. I'm hungry," he replies. "Let's grab some food first."

Grab some food on PAGE 24.
Follow the passenger to PAGE 54.

You have to close the locker. You crawl along the floor of the boat. Twenty-foot waves toss the boat into the air. Water crashes around you.

You have to stand to press down on the lid. Done! As you turn around, a wave smashes into you. It knocks you overboard.

You're in the ocean!

Huge waves toss you underwater. You twist and turn in the churning sea. When you struggle to the surface, you can't see the lifeboat!

You scream, but another wave drives icy water into your mouth.

I'm going to drown, you think in terror.

Then your arm bangs into something.

What is it? Find out on PAGE 89.

People are moaning all around you.

Then something makes you gag.

A skinny man is transforming right before your eyes. His skin is getting rougher — and scaly. His body blows up like a weather balloon. He looks like — a puffer fish!

Across from him, a young girl's body flattens out like a pancake. Her legs turn into arms. And — oh, gross — she's growing a *fifth* arm! She's morphing into a starfish!

You have got to be dreaming! You blink. But the incredible scene doesn't vanish.

"The Boss must have performed experiments on these people before we got here," you gasp.

Glenn's eyes are wide with terror.

The horror doesn't stop! One kid is turning into a red snapper. Another looks like a bluefish. "Hungry," he groans through a mouthful of razor-sharp choppers.

A thought hits you: Fish eat meat.

Gulp. *You're* meat.

Go to PAGE 72.

You hold your breath. Did you catch the pilot's attention?

The plane drops a parachute and flies off.

Yahoo! The pilot must have spotted you! They're dropping some kind of care package. Maybe a communication device.

The parachute seems to be headed for the center of the island. Excited, you race to the spot you expect it to land.

That's funny. You notice a sign in a clearing. It's written in a dozen different languages. You find the English part:

DANGER! YOU ARE TRESPASSING ON A RESTRICTED NUCLEAR TEST SITE. LEAVE AT ONCE!

You glance up. Your stomach squeezes when you realize what the parachute is really delivering. An atomic bomb!

Question: How are you and a bag of microwave popcorn alike?

Answer: You're both about to be nuked!

THE END

Inside the box are computer chips.

Something is wrong. Companies don't ship computer parts in dumpy little boats like this one.

Then the lightbulb goes on in your head. This crew must be smuggling stolen chips!

You close the door behind you. You sneak back to your bunk.

Oh, man, you think. I'm trapped on a ship full of crooks. And I'm totally at their mercy.

The next morning you pass the bridge. Through an open porthole you hear Klink talking to the captain.

"No one else could have broken the crate," Klink insists. "It must have been our little guest. Let me eliminate that pest."

Before you hear the captain's reply, a sailor strolls by. "Move along," he snaps at you. You obey quickly.

You pace by your bunk. Your heart pounds hard. Are they going to "eliminate" you? You hear footsteps coming below.

Klink and the captain confront you. "Did you break into the cargo hold last night?" the captain bellows at you.

Telling the truth could get you killed. But you know it pays to be honest. Think quick! What are you going to say?

If you say yes, go to PAGE 133.
If you say no, go to PAGE 135.

The dolphins swim you alongside a U.S. Navy cruiser. They leap and chirp to attract attention.

It works!

The dolphin who gave you the ride waits until the crew hauls you aboard. Then the creature swims away. You wave good-bye.

The ship drops you off in Hawaii. Your parents will pick you up in a week. You spend the time at the Marina Institute, learning to communicate with dolphins. You are fascinated by the incredible mammals. You could say you *flipped* for them. In fact, you become something of a dolphin *fin*-atic.

You and the sea creatures get along swimmingly. So no one is surprised when you grow up to become a marine biologist in

THE END.

You and Glenn go after the sneaky-looking passenger. You glance around. All clear. No sailors to
stop you. You dash through the huge silver door.

You find yourselves in an empty stairwell. You
head down and discover a corridor of storage clos-
ets.

"Well, it looks like that sailor was right," you
comment. "Nothing very interesting down here."

"Where did that guy go?" Glenn wonders.

You spot a light on under one door. "Shhh." You
hold a finger to your lips. You tiptoe to the door
and swing it open. Inside, the passenger kneels
over his black bag.

The man jumps up in surprise. Then a different
expression crosses his face. His eyes burn into
you.

"Get out!" he screams. "You're in terrible danger! Get off this ship any way you can!"

Turn to PAGE 14.

It's the guy who threatened to blow up the ship. Tom Bosco!

Sort of.

Only now his head sticks out of a giant turtle shell.

"This is your fault," Bosco snarls. "I'm a reptile because you turned me in!"

You're stunned to see him. It. Whatever.

"Hey," you gulp, feeling really guilty. "I'm sorry about what happened to you."

He points his front flipper at a distant wall, where a steel cage door is swinging open. "And I'm really sorry about what's *going* to happen to you," he growls.

Bosco yanks his head into his shell.

When you see what comes through the cage door you wish *you* had a shell. A very large shell.

Go to PAGE 4.

56

A shark's fin slices swiftly through the water.

This is bad, you think.

Then you spot two other sharks. This is *really* bad.

You stay as still as possible. You hope they don't notice you.

No such luck. They head straight toward you.

They're getting closer. You can see the lead shark's sleek gray body charging through the water. It's almost on top of you.

Punch it in the nose, you think. That will scare it off.

But you're weak with fear. You don't know if you can land a jab.

Then the shark dives. You can't see it anymore. You're so frightened you feel sick.

WHOOSH!

The shark leaps out of the water — right by your face!

Go to PAGE 91.

"Let's use the fish as bait," you decide. "Then we'll have all the fish we want."

Steve tears off a long strip of his shirt. You tie the remains of the fish to one end. You grip the other end and drop the fish over the side of the boat.

Pretty soon you feel a tug. Then the line is ripped out of your hands!

"Way to go, butterfingers," Bob sneers.

"I didn't drop it," you protest. But before you can say anything else, something bangs into the boat.

You peer over the side.

And freak.

A great white shark is ramming the lifeboat!

"It must have been attracted by the dead fish," Judy gasps.

The shark backs away. Then it swims like a missile at the raft. It hits nose-first and almost knocks over the boat.

The shark backs up and turns away again.

Maybe it's leaving, you hope.

Yeah. Sure it is.

Read what really happens on PAGE 74.

It's not a lobster — it's Glenn! He tripped and belly flopped into the water. Now he's back on his feet. He pulls ahead of you.

A ladder to the hatch is ten feet away. Now it's five. Glenn leaps up and grabs the ladder. He starts climbing.

"Hurry!" you scream.

He's halfway up. You step on the first rung. Faster, you think. Faster!

But you're not fast enough.

A five-foot-long pincer snaps on your leg.

You feel a searing pain.

The claw pulls you off the ladder.

Hmmm. When lobsters eat people, do they wear people bibs?

Unfortunately, you are about to find out!

THE END

You're saved! "It's me!" you cry. "We can hang on together until help comes."

"Keep away!" Glenn shouts.

What? You're stunned. What's wrong? you wonder.

You swim up to him. He's clutching a small piece of wood.

"This wood isn't big enough for both of us," he snarls.

Treading water, you stare at him. Your eyes widen in disbelief.

"Find your own wood," he yells, kicking at you.

"You would let me drown?" you gasp.

"If I let you hold on, we'll *both* drown," Glenn replies. "This way, one of us will survive. Me."

"Some pal you are," you snap. "Consider our friendship over!"

You wave your hand at him in disgust. You kick your legs hard to turn around toward the lifeboat.

The trouble is, it's about a half mile away.

You start swimming. And swimming. And swimming.

But you've got this *sinking* feeling you can't make it.

That's because you *are* sinking!

THE END

You climb on Glenn's shoulders and push up the trapdoor. Then you pull yourself through. A moment later, you're standing on top of the elevator car. Above you is the dark, creepy elevator shaft.

"The door is about ten feet up," you call down to Glenn. "We'll have to climb the cable to reach it."

You pull Glenn up through the trapdoor. He stands next to you on the roof of the car. "Can we climb this cable?" he asks nervously. "It's so greasy."

The steel cable *is* greasy. But it's the only way.

You climb up a few feet. Then you slip down a few feet. It's a slow, agonizing struggle to climb the ten slick feet. The work makes your arm muscles burn.

Finally you pull even with the double door. You stretch your upper body toward it while holding on to the cable with your legs. You try to pry the two doors apart with all your might.

Sweat pours off you. You're stretched like a rope between the doors and the cable.

You can't hold on much longer!

Go to PAGE 77.

"What's going on?" you demand.

Steve chuckles. "I told the guard you were escaping. In return, the chief promised to release me. All my problems are solved."

You don't understand. Then all of a sudden, you do. It all falls into place. "There was no ghost on the lifeboat," you exclaim. "*You* got rid of Judy and Hal."

Steve shrugs. "Sure. I made up the ghost story. And you helped make it believable. Hey, there wasn't enough food and water for all of us. I did it to survive. And now I'm going to get rid of you for the same reason. Nothing personal."

The chief points to Bob. "Into the cage with *wallabingbang*."

You don't like the sound of that.

Armed tribesmen lead Bob away.

The chief turns to you. "You are to be tossed to *zabamii*. Much worse than *wallabingbang*."

Today is not your lucky day.

The tribesmen march you to a small lake. The surface of the water seems alive with movement. Dread grows in you as you understand exactly what *zabamii* are.

Yikes!

Crocodiles!

Go to PAGE 118.

You're not sure Bosco is telling you the truth. And you don't want to deal with the shark-man.

"Head for the rope!" you yell to Glenn.

Before the startled shark-man can react, you're halfway up the rope. The shark can't climb — it has no arms. Frustrated, it gnashes its hideous teeth.

You pull yourself onto the catwalk. "Yeah! We made it!" you howl. Glenn is pale, but manages a small smile.

You run to the end of the catwalk, open the door, and step into a small hallway. The only way to exit is by elevator. You press the button.

"I hope nobody's in there," Glenn worries.

Your stomach is doing flip-flops. You don't want to get caught in this dead end either.

A minute later the elevator doors open.

The car is empty. Whew! You frantically press buttons. The car rises. Then stops short.

"The elevator stalled!" Glenn shrieks. "We're stuck!"

You press all the buttons. But the elevator doesn't move.

You glance up. There's a small, square trapdoor built into the car's ceiling.

You've seen enough action movies to know that the door opens into the elevator shaft. But can you make like an action hero?

Take action on PAGE 60.

If only I had a compass, you think. I wonder if I can make one.

You remember making a compass in science class. It had something to do with a magnet.

Hey, wait a minute! You can make a compass using that souvenir magnet you picked up on the *Finatic*.

You don't remember any magnet? Then check out PAGE 9. Right now.

Checked? Then you also found the paper clip in your pocket.

You break off part of the clip and magnetize it by rubbing one end against the magnet. You fill up half a coconut with seawater. You find a leaf in the canoe and float it on the water. Finally you place the clip on the leaf. The magnetized end of the clip points north.

You grin. Cool! You're a regular Thomas Edison!

Now you know for sure which way is which. But which way should you go?

If you paddle west toward Japan, go to PAGE 122.

If you paddle east toward America, go to PAGE 129.

You start hitting the numbers on the lock.

But the light stays red.

Big surprise.

There are ten different digits on the lock. The number of possible combinations is astronomical. And you don't even know how many numbers are in the code.

It would probably take you a century to hit them all.

You have about, oh, one minute.

This wasn't the greatest choice. By the time you realize you should have tried the eel, it's too late.

The piranha is ready to have a meal.

With Glenn as the main course.

And you as dessert.

THE END

You sneak up to the bridge on the top deck. This is where the communication equipment is located. You hope you'll be able to call ashore for help.

You and Glenn hide behind a high coil of ropes. You wait until the officer on duty has stepped out. You rush onto the bridge, your heart racing.

Oh, man. No phones. You slam your fist down in disgust. Then you notice a bank of closed-circuit TV monitors.

The screens show views of different parts of the ship. One view is of a door. You make out a sign on it: C DECK CREW ONLY. On the screen, a crew-woman opens the door with a key.

You poke Glenn. "I think C Deck is the lowest deck. We should see if that's where The Room is."

Glenn sighs. "Do we have to?"

"Yes! We have to find The Room," you insist. "It's our only chance to save all the passengers and ourselves from being transformed into monsters."

A bunch of keys dangle on the wall. You grab the one labeled C DECK.

You head down to C Deck. You slip the key into the door, unlock it, and step through.

Find out what you're stepping into on PAGE 41.

As you watch the paper sink, Fisher bursts into the kitchen.

"Where's the formula?" he demands. "Tell me or I'll kill you."

You smirk. "If you do that, you'll never find it."

Fisher advances toward you and Glenn. You feel your bravado waver. Glenn sweats beside you.

A sailor dashes into the kitchen. "The captain wants you," she informs Fisher.

Fisher follows her out. "I'm keeping my eye on you little punks," he bellows over his shoulder.

Once Fisher leaves, you reach into the ice cream maker.

"Get your hands away from there!" Henri, the head chef, rushes toward you. Straightening his white chef's hat, he orders you out.

You pace in the dining room, hoping to sneak back into the kitchen. You need that sheet of paper. It's your only bargaining chip with Fisher. Soon passengers file in for dinner.

"We might as well eat," Glenn suggests. He snags a table.

You're too bummed out to eat more than a few bites.

For dessert the waiters bring out a huge ice cream cake. And you suddenly regain your appetite.

Because you know how to get the formula back.

Find out how on PAGE 36.

The creatures come at you. You don't think you can outswim them. So you jump up to grab the steam pipe.

No! You can't reach it.

The lobsters are closing in! Their huge pincers snap together. You know they can crush you — tear through your body.

"Give me a boost!" you scream at Glenn. He cups his hands. You put your foot on them, then leap onto his shoulder.

Glenn starts teetering. You grab for the pipe.

And miss.

"Stand still!" you shout.

Glenn freezes. You bend your knees and jump.

Your fingers wrap around the pipe!

You do a chin-up and get your arms around the pipe. It starts to bend under your weight. But the pipe is really hot. It's burning your hands. You can't hold on!

Fall to PAGE 126.

You and the fish creatures spill out of the cage. The piranha-man nips at you. But you easily out-run him.

Where is The Room? you wonder as other fish-people stumble by.

Just then a woman passes you. She has reddish fins on the sides of her back. She's turning frantically in circles.

You nudge Glenn. "What's wrong with the salmon-lady?" As you watch her, she runs toward an exit sign like she knows where she's going.

Glenn points at her. "Follow that fish!"

"How come?" you ask.

"Salmon always return to where they were born," Glenn explains.

"So?" you ask.

"She was 'born' in The Room. She'll return there to give birth."

"Glenn!" you cry. "You're a genius!"

You tail the salmon-lady. She leads you through a maze of corridors deep down in the ship.

She pushes through a door. A sign on it reads, NO ONE ADMITTED TO THE ROOM!

This is it! You found it!

Go in on PAGE 90.

Running along Fisher's back is a narrow golden fin.

Well, you always thought he was a fishy character.

The sailors haul Mrs. Bass, Fisher, and the *Finatic*'s crew onto the coast guard ship. Other sailors stay on board to steer the ship back to California. When it docks, the mutant passengers are sent to live in aquariums around the country.

Except for the extra-large turtle named Tom Bosco. It turns out Bosco is a lawyer from San Diego.

"It's your fault I got changed," he tells you. "You owe me! I'm not going to be put on display. I'm staying with you. Or I'll sue your whole family!"

Your folks are a little put off by Bosco. But they're good sports. They let you take Bosco home with you. You keep him in the garage. Bosco repays you for his tank and turtle food — he does your parents' taxes and helps you sue the cruise line to get your money back.

Wow! you think. Who would have realized lawyers make such great pets!

THE END

The cold water is a shock to your system. Your muscles tense up. And as the ship sinks, it creates a powerful suction. You feel it dragging you down.

Fight for your life! you order yourself.

You kick away from the handrail with all your strength. You shoot to the surface. You breathe in great gulps of air.

Treading water, you gaze around. The gigantic ship is gone. The sea is filled with debris.

You can't believe it all happened so fast.

You swivel around. And spot something to your left.

A lifeboat! But it's so far away. Maybe there's another one closer.

You twist around to the right. You spot someone bobbing in the water even farther in the distance.

It's Glenn! He seems to be holding on to something. It's keeping him above water! Maybe it can do the same for you too.

If you swim to Glenn, go to PAGE 78.
If you swim to the lifeboat, go to PAGE 82.

You're a shrimp!

The good news is that you're a jumbo shrimp. And that you have feet.

The bad news is that you have a shell and no backbone.

Mrs. Bass has no trouble scooping you up. She places you in a cage with other fish-people. It's packed like sardines. That's because everyone in there *is* a sardine. One of them calls you Shrimpy.

Even fish-people laugh at you.

Imagine what humans would do.

You can never return to your old life. So you volunteer to help build Mrs. Bass's underwater city.

She turns you down.

"I have other plans for you," Mrs. Bass decides. Uh-oh. She looks hungry.

You feel a shiver run through you as she twists open a large jar of cocktail sauce.

THE END

Sweat pops out on your forehead. "We have to get out of here. Before it's feeding time at the aquarium," you tell Glenn.

You both tug on the door. But it won't budge.

Your eyes land on a kid wriggling on the cement floor. She's becoming an electric eel. You know that fish is totally deadly.

Behind you is a little old man with thinning white hair. As you watch, his jaw fills with piranha teeth. They look like serrated steak knives. You know — the kind that can cut through a tomato *and* a metal can.

A nature program you saw once told you piranhas can eat a whole cow in two minutes. So this giant one could probably scarf you down in twenty seconds.

Oh, man! You have to get out of this cage.

Wait! The electric eel! Maybe you can use it to short out the cage's electronic lock. Of course, the eel might short *you* out. Permanently.

On the other hand, you can press the numbers on the lock and hope you hit the code that opens it.

You don't have much time to decide. Which is it?

If you use the electric eel to open the door, go to PAGE 44.

If you to try to hit the code to open the door, go to PAGE 64.

You must be hearing an echo. Obviously the big object is the ship. Water can play tricks with sound.

You paddle as fast as you can. In the thick fog you still can't make out the white object. But it has to be a ship. You are so excited at the idea of being rescued that you manage to paddle even harder.

CRASH!

Your canoe smashes into a sharp chunk of ice.

You hit an iceberg! That's what the white object is.

Freezing water floods the craft. You find yourself treading icy water.

But chill out. Sometimes life can be pretty cold. And this is certainly one cold

END.

The shark circles the boat.

Desperate, you grab a paddle and try to whack the shark's face.

You swing. And miss.

Strike one.

The shark thrashes in the water. It's tricky to hit. You aim.

And miss again.

Strike two.

"Do something!" Bob shouts.

"Why don't *you* try something?" you fume. He makes you so mad, you swing wildly.

And smack the shark right on its nose with a *thwack*! The creature turns tail and disappears under the waves.

You can't believe it! You fought off a man-eating shark!

"Home run!" you exclaim. Steve pounds you on the back. Even Bob shakes your hand. Everybody whoops and celebrates.

Too soon.

Something lifts the raft a foot in the air. "What the . . . ?" you cry. A second later the craft flips upside down.

All four of you tumble into the water. And come face-to-face with the shark. Its massive jaws open. . . .

Whoops! Looks like this is actually strike three . . . and you're out — of luck!

THE END

"I'm sure that guy is harmless," you declare.

You decide not to bother the crew. You'd freak out everyone over nothing.

You and Glenn head up to the deck. You make your way to the front of the ship. You stare out at the enormous expanse of ocean.

"Cool!" You lean over the railing and watch the waves break against the side of the ship as it races through the water. The brisk breeze ruffles through your hair. It makes your skin tingle.

"This cruise is the best!" you exclaim.

A second later a tremendous explosion rocks the ship. It shakes so hard you almost fall over the side.

Smoke pours across the deck. Flames shoot high into the air.

You and Glenn stare at each other in horror. That guy was crazy, but he was telling the truth.

He *did* have a bomb!

Sink down to PAGE 45.

You squirm through a narrow passage in total darkness. Panic rises in your chest. You feel as if the walls are closing in on you.

Get a grip, you tell yourself. This is better than feeling the lizard's teeth ripping through you.

Soon the passage opens onto a large chamber. Sunlight shines through a hole in the roof. It must lead outside!

You start to climb up when you see something. And gasp!

Go to PAGE 110.

With one last mega-effort, you try to pry apart the doors.

"Aaarghh!" you grunt. You slide open the door a foot and a half. You pull yourself through.

You did it!

Glenn slowly makes his way up the cable. You pull him through the door. You both collapse, exhausted. But you can't waste time on the floor. You stagger to your feet and step outside. You suck in the salty air. You're back on C Deck.

Blech! You're covered in axle grease and soaked in sweat. To cool off, you stride across the deck to the railing. You lean over, staring down at the frothy waves.

"Great job," Glenn cries. He slaps you on the back.

Oops.

He smacked you too hard. Your greasy body slides over the rail.

Whoooa! When you hit the sea, you slice deep underwater. You push yourself to the surface. You wipe the water out of your eyes.

You glance up. Glenn is up on the top deck. You see the horrified expression on his face. The ship glides slowly away.

Making like an action hero is slippery business. Guess this is one happy ending that slipped away.

THE END

You swim toward Glenn. You would rather be with your friend than with a bunch of strangers.

But the cold water makes it tough-going. Your arms tire quickly. Your chest muscles burn.

But you swim on. You have to. You're swimming for your *life*. Waves smack against you, sending water up your nose.

Glenn still seems so far away. You don't know if you can make it. You remember swimming far out into the ocean at the beach. Back then you panicked when you saw how far away the shore was.

And there's no shore here. Anywhere. In any direction.

You put your head down and plow through the water. Just keep going, you think. Stroke . . . stroke . . .

You glance up. Glenn is only a few hundred yards away!

You're within shouting distance.

"Glenn!" you scream. "Hey, buddy! I'm coming over there!"

Go to PAGE 59.

Turtles! Standing right in front of the hatch! Not the little ones you keep in a box. These guys are humongous.

But what's even more horrifying are the human heads sticking up out of the hard green shells.

The turtles shuffle slowly toward you. You and Glenn back up.

"What happened to you?" Glenn blurts.

"We were transformed in The Room," a turtle with a mustache declares.

"We were passengers on an earlier cruise," the other turtle explains. "The Boss changed people into something part human, part sea creature."

"The first experiments didn't work well," the mustached turtle adds. "The results were more human than animal. Those people became the ship's crew. Others turned out less human. Like us. The Boss is trying for the perfect blend. Half human and half sea creature."

Your eyes widen in shock. What a terrifying story!

And you and Glenn are trapped in the middle of it!

A third turtle lurches toward you.

You gasp!

Flip out on PAGE 55.

For some reason, you trust Bosco. Maybe it's because you once had a pet turtle.

You face the shark. Saliva drips from its mouth. It can't seem to speak. But you read its body language loud and clear. It wants to eat you.

Getting past this monster will be hard.

Hard. That's it! Bosco's shell is hard!

You kneel down beside Bosco and whisper your plan. He agrees.

"Help me pick up Bosco," you order Glenn.

You get Bosco upright. You and Glenn push Bosco toward the door. You use the turtle's shell like a shield.

The shark bites down on Bosco. But the shell is hard as a rock.

You strain to keep the turtle between you and the vicious fish. It's only a few more yards to the cage door and safety.

"Now!" you shout. Together you slam Bosco's shell against the shark. This pushes him away from the steel door.

"Go!" you scream as you dive through the cage door. You pull it shut behind you. The door locks.

"Hello." An unexpected voice greets you.

Go to PAGE 136.

"I will make this recipe," Henri declares. You and Glenn follow him into the kitchen.

Henri follows the recipe exactly. He mixes together two cups of mayonnaise and one-half cup of pickles, plus one-eighth cup of salt and one-sixteenth cup of pepper. He takes a lick. *"Magnifique!"*

He holds out the spoon for you and Glenn to taste. "That's good," you comment.

"Good? Ha! It is the most superb tartar sauce I have ever tasted! This recipe is worth a fortune!" Henri raves.

He turns to you and Glenn. "Become my partners. We will go into the tartar sauce business together."

The terrible experiments Bosco ranted about? They were *cooking* experiments!

Your tartar sauce company is a worldwide success. You become rich and eventually you hire the pathetic Fisher to work in your factory. . . .

As a pickle unpacker.

THE END

82

You swim toward the lifeboat. It's closer than Glenn. Once aboard, you'll get them to pick him up too.

It's hard to swim with your clothes weighing you down. And the water is so cold. Halfway there, you almost give up.

Don't wimp out, you tell yourself.

Finally, you reach the lifeboat. Several pairs of hands stretch toward you and haul you up.

You collapse onto a seat. Your teeth chatter. You're exhausted and freezing. But you're alive!

You glance back toward Glenn. Good! Another lifeboat has picked him up. They disappear into the fog.

You gaze at your shipmates. There are four teenagers on the fifteen-foot-long boat. They introduce themselves.

Bob is kind of heavy. You don't like the way he sneers at you. Judy wears a baseball hat with her school's name on it. She looks like an honor roll geek — the ultraserious type. Steve is a regular guy and the friendliest. Hal is quiet and seems frightened. All four were on the *Finatic* as part of a school trip. But they aren't really friends.

You gaze out at the ocean. You don't see any lifeboats anymore.

You're all alone now.

Go to PAGE 96.

Glenn shouts in pain and collapses.

"You're, you're . . . the Boss!" you stammer.

Mrs. Bass removes her flowered scarf. You gasp.

She has gills!

"Yes," she jeers. "I first used fish DNA on myself. But I needed more subjects for my experiments. I had to perfect the transformation process."

"B-but why?" you stutter.

"To create a race of fish-people," she replies. "They will build me an underwater city, which I will rule. We'll live on the ocean floor. You humans can have the surface. It stinks up there."

You stare at her. She's obviously insane.

And very dangerous.

She picks up another syringe and comes at you.

Go to PAGE 39.

The tortoise swims through the ocean. With you along for the ride. You don't know where it's going. But you hope it will get there soon.

Day and night the reptile's large flippers sweep it steadily forward. Its strength amazes you. It hardly seems to notice you're there. "Just don't dive, okay?" you whisper to it, clutching its shell.

Three days later you spot land. The tortoise swims to shore. You jump off.

"Thanks," you tell the tortoise. It shuffles away to lay its eggs in the sand. You watch it go, grateful for the ride.

Hey! People! There are two men and a woman strolling toward you. You stagger up to the woman and ask her where you are.

"These are the Galápagos Islands," she answers. She's with a group of scientists studying the island's amazing wildlife.

Guess what? They need an assistant.

You apply for the job and are hired on the spot. The researchers radio your parents to ask their permission. Your folks think working with scientists is a fantastic idea. Hey, it's educational!

Wow! Scientifically speaking, this has turned out to be the best vacation ever!

THE END

Are you NUTS?

Drink seawater?

Get real!

You might as well swallow a bottle of poison.

You're obviously a landlubber. Any sailor worth his salt would tell you that saltwater dehydrates you.

Terminally.

Spill the water, go back to PAGE 108, and choose again.

Sheesh!

Go to PAGE 108.

The door is opening! Glenn's eyes bug out. So do yours. You shove him toward the bathroom. "Let's hide in there," you whisper.

You slip into the tiny bathroom and lock the door behind you. You put your ear to the door and hear a man's voice. It's Fisher's!

"I've got the hundred thousand dollars in this bag," you hear him say. "Give me the envelope and the money is yours."

Another voice cries, "The envelope's empty!"

"Search the cabin for the paper," Fisher demands. "I need that information. My operation depends on it."

What operation? you wonder. What's that formula for? And what could "TS" stand for? Transformed species? Titanium ship?

The bathroom doorknob jiggles. "The bathroom's locked!" a man yells.

"Break down the door," Fisher orders.

WHAM! Something rams the door. You know the lock won't hold.

How do we get out of here? you wonder. You spot a small porthole in one wall. But you're not sure it's big enough to squeeze through. On the other wall is a metal laundry chute.

Which way out? Decide — fast!

If you try to escape through the porthole, go to PAGE 35.

If you try to get away by the laundry chute, go to PAGE 40.

All four of you bail water frantically. The rain comes down in sheets. Water reaches your ankles.

You keep scooping out the water. Your arms ache. But you know if you stop, the lifeboat will sink.

Hours later the rain slows down.

"I've never seen so much rain," you tell Steve. "That must have been a monsoon."

His lips move in response. But the wind whips away his words.

The wind? Uh-oh.

The wind blows stronger. It starts howling. The waves get higher.

That rainstorm wasn't a monsoon. *This* is a monsoon!

The storm rages around you. You all huddle in the bottom of the boat. "Please don't capsize," you murmur.

Then you notice the food-and-water locker. No one closed it. The water container could fall out. All the drinking water you collected would spill away!

You're closest to the locker. But if you get up, you might be tossed overboard. What should you do?

Get up to close the lid? Go to PAGE 49.
Stay seated? Go to PAGE 92.

Your back burns. It's on fire! You turn around and see what caused the pain.

Mrs. Bass has transformed. Into a jellyfish!

Her hair is a snarling mass of stingers. The tentacles snaked under your shirt and stung you.

A ten-foot-long tentacle brushes your hand. OWWWWW!

Angry red welts form on your fingers. Another tentacle stings your arm. Then your cheek.

While you scratch your itchy skin, Mrs. Bass grabs another syringe and jabs you with it.

You fall to the ground. Your head swims. Your bones begin to ache. Your insides are burning.

You glance down. Your arm is turning gray. Your back is curving. Now your skin is getting crusty and thick.

Oh, no!

Go to PAGE 71.

Your fingers close around the object. You pull it toward you.

It's a life buoy from the *Finatic*! It must have blown off the lifeboat during the storm.

You slip it around your chest. Giant waves toss you like a toy. But the life buoy keeps you from sinking.

You're still terrified. But now you feel a glimmer of hope.

All night the storm beats against you. All you think of is staying alive — minute by minute, hour by hour.

When morning arrives, the winds die down. The storm has ended.

I made it, you think gleefully. I survived!

But so what? You're floating in the ocean. Probably miles from the lifeboat.

You're so scared, you start to laugh. "Where is everybody?" you shout.

Then you spot something coming your way.

Hey! You're not alone after all.

A shark has come along to keep you company.

Go to PAGE 56.

You follow the salmon-lady inside.

Calming yourself, you examine the clean white room. It's filled with microscopes and tons of high-tech lab equipment. Shelves are lined with rows of fluid-filled test tubes. The labels read SHARK DNA, TORTOISE DNA, ROCKFISH DNA. There are hundreds of tubes, each with the genes of a different fish.

You stare at tiny fish floating in jars of formaldehyde. You gasp.

Some have human features.

Wow! This must be where the Boss conducts horrible experiments.

But who is the Boss? Why does he want to do these horrible experiments?

At the back of the lab is a door marked PRIVATE.

You tingle with fear and excitement. You're certain you'll find the answers, and maybe this Boss guy, in the next room.

You pull open the door.

What you see inside is beyond belief.

Believe on PAGE 132.

"Aagh!" you shriek.

The shark jumps at you and —

Nuzzles your cheek!

Your eyes widen in astonishment. You can't believe it.

It's not a shark — it's a dolphin!

Now you can see that there are lots of dolphins swimming beside you. They chirp and leap into the air. They want to play.

This is so cool!

After a while they swim off. They stop. Then they swim back to you. They do this a few times before it hits you.

The dolphins want you to follow them.

One swims to your side. You hug its midsection. The super-smart mammal pulls you at incredible speed through the sea. This is the greatest water ride ever!

Soon you notice a dark speck in the distance.

A ship!

Swim with the dolphins over to PAGE 53.

The boat is rocking too much to move. You're afraid you'll tip over into the water. So you stay put.

The storm lasts all night. By morning the sky clears up.

Luckily, the water and food didn't fall out of the locker.

But unluckily, the storm drove you a hundred miles from where the *Finatic* sunk. Even if a rescue party was looking for you, they wouldn't know your location now.

And to make matters worse, the rain soaked the biscuits. Most of them dissolved.

"We can only eat half a biscuit a day," Bob announces.

"Is this your lost-at-sea diet?" you joke. "You'll make millions on the infomercial."

Nobody laughs.

Night after night, nightmares wake you. You lie watching the fog drift across the water and over the boat. Sometimes you think you see the shape of a man. You also hear weird noises.

Is it a ghost? you wonder. Or is hunger making you hallucinate?

One morning you spot some kind of island in the distance. At least, you hope it's an island. It could be another hallucination.

Only one way to find out. "Land!" you cry hoarsely.

Check it out on PAGE 29.

You need food. And a whale is the Big Mac of sea creatures — a supersize order of meat and blubber.

You paddle slowly toward the huge creature. It floats calmly in the water. It doesn't seem to notice you.

You raise the flare gun. You aim and press the trigger.

The orange flare shoots out. It sputters through the air and slams into the side of the whale.

Then it bounces harmlessly off the whale's thick hide. The flare sizzles in the water beside the creature.

Uh-oh. *Now* the whale seems to have noticed you.

Paddle to PAGE 11.

You rip through the black garbage bag. You crawl out. Glenn follows, brushing orange peel off his shirt.

You scramble to your feet. You discover you're in the ship's trash collection area. It's a warehouse-size room full of garbage bags.

You're not alone.

Standing nearby are the two crew members who carried the bag downstairs. "Hey," one exclaims. "These are the kids Fisher told us to get rid of."

The other sailor cackles. "You've heard of compact cars and compact discs? How about compact kids?"

You don't get the joke.

Then they drag you to a door labeled COMPACTOR ROOM.

Now you get the joke. But you're not laughing.

They toss you into the room and slam the door. Before you have time to be afraid, a large steel plate starts moving down from the ceiling.

"This can't be happening!" you cry. But it is.

You and Glenn hold up your arms to stop the mammoth plate. But of course you can't. It pushes you flat against the floor.

Your hopes of escaping are about to be totally crushed!

THE END

You let the water dribble out of your hand.

You're no fool. Drinking seawater will bring you a painful death.

But you *are* thirsty. Without fresh water you're doomed. You stare gloomily at the dark clouds hovering in the distant sky.

Dark clouds! Those are *rain* clouds!

You point at them. "We have to paddle toward those clouds!" you holler.

Bob sneers. "That's stupid. We can't waste energy rowing toward some clouds."

But Judy backs you up. So you and she grab the oars and paddle toward the clouds. As you get closer, you feel a few drops. Then it starts pouring! Water! Wonderfully wet water!

You open the water container so rain fills it. Pretty soon, the water container is brimming.

Then the lifeboat is brimming.

Uh-oh. It's flooded with rainwater!

Go to PAGE 87.

Everyone on the boat stares glumly out to sea. No one speaks.

I have to break this downer mood, you think. Or I'm going to go nuts. "Do you think the cruise will give us a refund?" you joke.

Bob glares at you. "This isn't funny. We have to figure out how to survive until we're rescued."

"Who made you captain?" you shoot back.

Bob lunges across the lifeboat at you. Steve and Hal hold him back. The boat shakes so much, it almost tips over.

"Stop it!" Judy orders. "We have to stick together. Or we're doomed."

This calms everyone down. You glare at Bob and sit back. "What a jerk!" you mutter.

Hal searches the boat. There is a small supply of biscuits and water in a metal container. He also finds two paddles and a flare gun with a single flare.

"What do you think caused the explosion?" Steve asks.

"Must have been the boiler," Hal suggests.

You don't want to tell them the truth. If they discover you could have stopped the explosion, they might throw you overboard.

You gaze out at the horizon, feeling very stupid.

The lifeboat bobs up and down. Up and down. Up and . . .

You're also feeling very sick.

Bob over to PAGE 13.

You polish off the fish. Yum! Only now you really wish you had some more. . . .

The next day, you stare into the ocean. Your mouth waters as you imagine fresh, tasty seafood. You watch a fish surfacing in the shadow of the raft. You have an idea.

You grab Judy's cap. Dragging the hat through the water, you scoop up the fish!

"Come and get it!" you cheer. You lay out the fish.

"You're taking too much," Bob accuses Judy.

"You already had your share," she retorts.

Steve gets angry. "You're both so selfish." He shakes his head. "There are just too many of us and too little food."

You fish with Judy's hat the rest of the day. But you don't catch anything. Meanwhile everyone's bickering. You notice that the vibes on the boat are getting worse and worse.

That night a sound wakes you. You think you see a shape moving in the fog. Is it the ghost? You're too groggy to move.

You hear a groan, followed by a muffled cry. Then a splash.

I must be dreaming, you think. You close your heavy lids.

The next morning you wake up to discover — Judy is missing.

Go to PAGE 26.

He has scales! Running across part of his chest and back are . . . shiny gray fish scales.

Your stomach lurches at the sight. Glenn covers his mouth.

The scaly guy changes his shirt, then the creepy crewmen leave.

"What's with those guys?" Glenn is so freaked out his voice squeaks. You don't blame him — you're freaked out too!

Your brain reels as you try to think of an explanation. But you can't think of one.

"There must be a connection between those two guys and what's going on in The Room that Bosco mentioned," you figure. "That's why we have to find it. That's where we'll learn what is going on here. And how we can stop it."

You and Glenn creep out of the crew's quarters. Glancing around, you notice extra-large garbage bags piled by the ship's stern. They are fenced off from the rest of the deck.

"Let's hide in those garbage bags," you suggest. "After everyone goes to sleep, we can sneak out and search for The Room."

"I have a better idea," Glenn declares. "I think we should go to the top deck. That's where the bridge is. We can probably find a phone there — and call for help."

If you follow Glenn's idea, go to PAGE 65.
If you stick with your plan, go to PAGE 37.

You glance up at the sound. Your heart skips a beat. A plane!

The plane flies so low, you hear its engines.

"Look!" You point up at the sky. "A plane! We have to attract its attention!"

Bob and Steve start yelling. They wave their arms wildly. Bob yanks off his shirt and flaps it like a flag.

The plane is almost overhead. You have only a few seconds to catch the pilot's eye.

You screech at the top of your lungs. But the pilot is a thousand feet away. He can't hear you.

Your heart pounds. You know you may not get this chance to be rescued again.

How can you make the people in the plane notice you?

If you fired the flare gun at the whale, go to PAGE 104.

If you didn't fire the flare gun, go to PAGE 30.

The island is too far away. You would never make it. Besides, those may not be friendly people over there. You decide to concentrate on improving your life here.

For example, your leaf bed isn't much use in the rain. You definitely need better shelter.

You start exploring. You discover a small mountain near the center of the island. At its base is a cave. This becomes your new, rent-free home.

You don't venture deep inside. The bats make sure of that.

Next on your agenda: a better diet. You're awfully sick of being a vegetarian. You decide to make a spear for hunting.

You break off a tree branch. Using a jagged stone, you trim the branch into a sharp spear. Finally you get it just right.

One evening you hear loud hissing outside your cave.

You peek out. Whoa! A seven-foot-long lizard sits inches from the entrance. It looks like a Komodo dragon. These babies can tear a person to shreds!

Should you fight it with your spear? Or retreat deeper into your cave?

If you fight the dragon, go to PAGE 106.
If you retreat, go to PAGE 109.

Over the next few days, you discover you're stranded on a deserted island. Luckily, it holds plenty of edible fruits and berries. They're tasty but get pretty boring — day after day after day . . .

"I could sure go for a burger." The voice makes you jump.

"Who said that?" you demand. Then you flush with embarrassment.

You said that. It's been so long since you heard the sound of your own voice, you didn't recognize it.

"I'm glad no one caught me," you say. "Hey, I'm doing a lot of talking out loud." You shake your head. "I just did it again. I'm *still* doing it. Am I going crazy?"

Then you shrug. "Nah, I just have no one to talk to."

You don't think you can stand the solitude much longer. Then you spot smoke rising above the island across the bay.

If there's fire . . . there must be . . . people!

Think! How can you get over there?

Or maybe it's just too dangerous. Maybe you should just stay put.

If you build a boat to get to the other island, go to PAGE 105.

If you hang tight, go to PAGE 100.

You stare hard at the dark bump on the horizon. That is no whale. Your heart pumps hard with excitement. You grin broadly.

You and Steve grab the oars and start paddling. As you get closer, you make out not one but *two* islands! The one on the left is a little smaller than the one on the right.

You can hardly wait to walk on land. Soon you hear surf pounding on the two islands' beaches.

Without warning, the bow of the lifeboat smacks into a large submerged rock. The boat's momentum sends you flying over the side and into the ocean.

You swim to the surface. You gasp for breath. You're totally disoriented. You flail in the water. "Help!" you cry.

You gaze around for the boat. But it's gone. It must have sunk, you realize. There's no sign of Bob and Steve. Did they drown?

You have to swim to one of the islands now. The island on the left is closer. But you feel a current pushing you to the island on the right. Which island should you head for?

If you swim to the island on the left, go to PAGE 27.

If you swim to the island on the right, go to PAGE 111.

It's tough work gutting all those pounds of fish. Day after day after day. But you don't care. You're (mostly) warm, (relatively) safe, and (usually) fed.

Three months later you arrive home. After all you've been through, you've never been so happy to be around your folks and friends. You want to hug everyone. And hang out with them day and night. But the odd thing is, they don't want to be close to you.

At all.

Not even in the same room.

Because no matter how much you wash, you still smell like fish.

And there's no two ways around it: That really stinks!

THE END

Too bad you already used the flare gun. You have no way to catch the pilot's eye. As the plane disappears in the distance, you collapse onto a seat. Now you're sure you'll never be rescued.

Which means any one of you could be the ghost's next victim.

If you don't starve first. . . .

The boat drifts aimlessly. At night you try to stay awake in case the ghost returns. The lack of sleep is getting to you.

You, Steve, and Bob hardly talk to each other. Anything you do gets on each other's nerves. So you just stare at the horizon, hoping to spot a ship.

One morning you happen to glance at Bob.

"What are you looking at?" he challenges.

"Your ugly face," you reply.

"I'll show you ugly," he shoots back.

"Good comeback, jerk," you sneer.

"I've spotted land," Steve announces.

Bob ignores Steve. "Oh, and that's a smart answer?" he snaps.

Hey — wait a sec. You stare at Steve. Did you hear him right?

He's laughing hysterically.

"Land!" he yells again.

Go to PAGE 102.

You figure building a boat shouldn't be too hard. You saw someone do it in a movie about a shipwrecked sailor.

You hack down some skinny trees with a jagged rock. Then you tear off some vines. You use them to lash the trees together. You find a piece of bark to use as a paddle.

You wipe sweat from your face. Phew! That was harder than you expected.

You haul the raft down to the beach. You wade past the breakers. Then you hop aboard.

Cool! You're a master boat builder!

But after you paddle about a hundred yards, the vines unknot. The whole boat falls apart.

You slide into the water.

Agh! A riptide catches you. You can't fight it! You flail around. But it's useless. The undertow drags you down. It sends you out to sea.

It looks as if the tide has finally turned against you.

Oh, well. Next time just go with the flow, dude!

THE END

You're not backing down from this mini Godzilla! If you don't fight it now, it could creep up on you later. Like when you're sleeping!

You grab the spear and swagger out of the cave.

The creature opens its jaws to scare you.

It works. You're definitely scared.

Rows of razor-sharp teeth fill the lizard's mouth. Its powerful bite can probably cut you in half.

You thrust the spear at its head. The lizard hisses and snaps its jaws. You have to time your jab perfectly. You want to shove the spear into the monster's open mouth.

There's your opening. Yes! Your spear goes in!

The lizard clamps down on the spear. *CRUNCH!* It bites down on the shaft. The force lifts you off the ground.

Yikes!

You're still clutching the spear when the lizard swallows it. *CHOMP!*

You've heard of armed to the teeth? This lizard has its teeth to your arm!

Looks like you and the lizard are growing more attached to each other with each passing moment!

THE END

You steer the canoe to the atoll. When you land, you drag the canoe onto the beach.

You stroll along the shore. You don't find anything. No people. Or any sign of them. But what's weird is that there aren't any animals, either. No birds. No insects. Just sand and trees.

You're about ready to give up when you hear the drone of an airplane. It's flying far above you.

"Hey! Down here!" you shout. You wave frantically, jumping up and down.

But did they see you?

Find out on PAGE 51.

108

You jump up. You stumble into Bob. "Watch it," he snaps.

As the fog lifts, you see Judy and Steve standing nearby. You glance around. "W-w-where's Hal?" you stammer.

You all peer into the dark water.

"I don't see him anywhere," Judy cries. She sounds panicky.

"How could he have fallen out?" you demand.

"This is going to sound nuts," Steve says. "But I . . . I think I saw a man on the boat. Wearing a hat with the words SS *Finatic* on it." Steve slumps down into the bottom of the boat. He seems totally weirded out.

"So who was he?" Bob asks sarcastically. "The ghost of a crewman who drowned on the *Finatic*? And he threw Hal overboard?"

"I — I don't know," Steve replies quietly.

You don't believe in ghosts. But you did hear that scraping sound and saw . . . *something*. No — it's too crazy. You decide not to say anything.

The next few nights no one spots any ghosts. But you run out of water.

You hang your head over the side of the raft and stare at the cool ocean water. It looks so delicious. So wet. You reach overboard and cup some seawater in your palm.

If you decide to drink the seawater, go to PAGE 85.

If you decide not to drink it, go to PAGE 95.

You might fight this giant lizard with a cannon. But not with a homemade spear.

You retreat.

You edge back into the cave. Uh-oh. The lizard follows you.

You keep backing up. But soon you back up against the cave wall. There's nowhere to go!

You stare at the lizard. It licks its chops.

The rough cave wall pokes your back. Sweat drips down your face. But a breeze dries the sweat quickly.

Hey, where's the breeze coming from? you wonder. You glance up.

You spot a small hole above a ledge. You find a foothold on the wall and climb up onto the ledge. You peer down.

The lizard snaps its jaws at you. But you pull your legs out of its reach. You wriggle headfirst through the hole.

Bye-bye, reptile!

Turn to PAGE 76.

You gaze at a man's skull.

Next to the head is a skeleton. And beside that is a large wooden box.

You hurry over and open the box. Inside you find an old book, worn with age.

It's the diary of an eighteenth-century pirate — the man whose remains you found. You read that he was shipwrecked on this island. How he lived the rest of his life here. And it tells of a treasure in the box's false bottom.

You can't believe it! Burning with excitement, you smash open the box. Jewels and gold doubloons spill out. It's stolen booty!

This must be worth millions!

Too bad you have nowhere to spend it. Because no one ever rescues you.

But the good news is, when you die of old age, you are the richest person on the island!

THE END

You head to the island on the right, swimming with the strong current. When you reach the beach, you search for Steve and Bob. No footprints in the sand. No bits of clothing.

Nothing.

You spend most of your time searching for fruits and berries to eat. You discover a stream with clean water to drink. Good thing the weather is warm and dry.

You can't help wondering if anyone is searching for you. If anyone cares. Some days you are overcome by major feelings of self-pity.

Then one day you explore a new section of the island. Your heart thumps. You spot a column of smoke rising into the sky.

The island must be inhabited after all!

You head in the direction of the smoke. Before long you come to a clearing in the jungle.

You find huts. But no people.

"Ow!" Something stings your back. It must be a mosquito. You shudder to make it fly off. It stings again. You turn around.

That's no mosquito.

That's a spear!

Go to PAGE 120.

112

You take the path that leads up the hill. It will provide better cover.

You reach the top of the hill. The island spreads out below you like a map. You spot a group of canoes on a secluded section of beach.

You glance down. The tribesmen finally figured out which path you took. They're racing up the hill. Steve leads them — that lousy traitor! But by now you have a huge head start.

You sprint down a twisting path. You stumble onto a beach lined by coconut trees. You race to the canoes.

Planning ahead, you shake down some coconuts and load a few dozen in the canoe for food. You use a sharp rock to knock holes in the other canoes so you can't be followed out to sea.

You don't have a moment to lose. The tribesmen will be down on the beach at any minute.

You drag the boat into the water. By the time your captors appear on the shore, you're rowing past the surf.

You turn around. "Later, losers!" you shout at them.

Paddle yourself to PAGE 121.

You all decide it would be safer to take the test.

The next day the tribesmen drag you out of the hut. They lead you to a large, steaming pit. Intense heat rises from it.

A rope stretches between poles on either side of the deadly pit. "You must cross the pit," the chief informs you.

Some test. In spite of the heat, chills race up your spine.

Bob goes first. He climbs up the pole and grabs the rope. He moves slowly, hand over hand. You can see his terrified expression. The sweat streaming down his face. You force yourself to watch.

Bob dangles over the middle of the pit. "I can't hold on!" he cries. "Aaahh!" He drops into the pit.

Gulp.

Steve is next. He has to be dragged to the pole.

He almost makes it. Then his hands slip. He falls into the pit.

Now it's your turn.

Take the test on PAGE 117.

You paddle toward the foghorn. Trouble is, it's hard to judge where the sound is coming from. You paddle slowly, first one way, then another. Finally you think you have it right.

A-WHOOOO!

The sound is coming right at you. Nice navigating! you congratulate yourself.

Then you notice the ship's bow. It's about ten feet away. Moving toward you at full speed.

You have no time to get out of the way!

"Help!" you shout.

SMASH!

The ship tears your canoe in half. You fly out, plunging into the freezing water. You're so cold, you can't even yell for help.

The stern of the ship glides past you. It's over, you think. I'm freezing to death. You shiver uncontrollably.

But the next moment something pulls you forward.

You're caught in a net!

Get dragged to PAGE 128.

You swing across the pit!

When you get to the other side, you let go of the rope. You tumble to the ground and roll for a few feet.

You made it! You passed the test!

No one ever passed the test before. The tribesmen are totally impressed. So they make you the new chief.

You enjoy the life of top banana. Eventually you marry and have kids. Everything seems perfect.

But one day the steaming pit explodes. Flames and lava shoot hundreds of feet into the air.

The pit was actually the top of a volcano! you realize.

As red-hot lava reaches your hut, you know that your reign as chief is over.

And that really burns you up!

THE END

116

You don't know what the test is. But it's probably a lot more painful than a math quiz. And harder to pass.

You all agree to escape.

You, Steve, and Bob huddle in the hut. "There's a guard in front of the door," you whisper. "Let's dig a hole under the back wall. We can escape after dark."

Bob nods. "We should head for the beach. I saw a canoe there. It's our only chance to get off this island."

Steve doesn't say anything. He seems really nervous.

"Don't worry," you promise him. "We're going to make it."

You dig under the back wall with an empty coconut. By midnight there's a hole large enough to squirm through.

Bob goes first. He barely squeezes through. Then it's your turn. In a few moments you're outside the hut. You're free!

You wait for Steve. And wait.

You stick your face into the hole. "Come on!" you whisper.

You turn back around. And discover you're surrounded by tribesmen.

Steve stands in the middle of them. Smiling.

Go to PAGE 61.

You climb up the pole. Your arms tremble with fear. Not good.

You have to get yourself under control, you order yourself. Or it's all over.

You gaze into the broiling pit. "Oh, man," you groan. If you fall in, you'll be a human barbecue.

You know there's no way you can make it across. Even if terror *wasn't* making you shake, you're weak from malnutrition and your near-death experiences. You scan the area, searching for a way out.

Then it hits you! You figure out how to pass the test.

The rope is knotted to the pole. You untie it. Down below, the tribesmen look confused by what you're doing.

You grip the rope in both hands. You breathe deeply. Here goes nothing, you think.

Then you let out a Tarzan yell. And push off from the pole.

Swing over to PAGE 115.

118

The lake is swarming with crocodiles!

"No!" you scream hysterically. You struggle against the tribesmen's grip. No use. Not only are these guys strong — you're surrounded by them. They drag you down to the lake.

You notice that the crocs are submerged partway in the water. Their heads stick out like flat stones. Hmmm. That gives you an idea. Maybe there *is* a way to save yourself.

You stop struggling. And when the guards release you, you run straight toward the lake. That confuses them.

You jump onto the head of the nearest croc. From its head, you leap onto another croc.

You cross the pond, hopping from one croc to the next. "In a while, crocodile!" you shout, laughing.

Leap to PAGE 43.

You race toward the ocean. You want to find that canoe Bob spotted on the beach.

As you run, you hear something zip past you. An arrow *thunks* against a tree.

They're firing at you! You gulp — and run faster.

You hear the surf crashing up ahead. The beach! Yes! You made a good choice! You break out of the forest and gaze at miles of beach.

But no canoe.

You smack yourself on the forehead. All Bob said was that he saw a canoe on the beach. But the beach surrounds the *entire island*. The canoe could be anywhere. On any stretch of sand.

While you marvel at your own stupidity, an arrow nicks your leg.

Whoa! Keep running! you remind yourself. Can't stop now!

You sprint over the sand. But soon one leg goes numb. Then your other leg. You fall to the ground. The numbness spreads over your body.

You realize the arrow was spiked with a paralyzing poison. You can't move. You can't breathe. You gaze at the beautiful beach, gasping for air.

Talk about a breathtaking view!

THE END

"Aaah!" You jump about two feet straight up in the air.

You've never seen anyone like the guy holding the spear. Rings dangle from his nose and earlobes.

"*Xenda grast inda santhi,*" the guy declares.

You don't understand. But you get the drift.

He wants you to move into the clearing. You don't argue.

He leads you to a hut. Inside, you discover Steve and Bob. They didn't drown! Your spirits rise at the sight of familiar faces.

"So they got you too," Steve observes.

Bob and Steve were captured a few days ago. They found out that the tribe's chief knows a little English. He learned it from a man who was shipwrecked here years ago.

"What are they going to do with us?" you ask anxiously.

As if to answer your question, the chief enters. "You take our test tomorrow," he declares. "Or die," he adds with a nasty smile. Your mouth drops open in shock as you watch him leave.

Bob is terrified. "I'm not taking any test."

"Yeah," Steve agrees. "We have to escape."

You don't know what the test is, but it's probably a killer. On the other hand, if you manage to escape, where will you go?

If you try to escape, go to PAGE 116.
If you take the test, go to PAGE 113.

"I did it!" you cheer. "I escaped! Whoo-hoo!"

But your celebration doesn't last.

I'm totally lost in the middle of the Pacific Ocean again, you soon realize.

You have to find land. You know Japan is to the west and America is to the east. But which direction is which?

Let's see, you think. The sun rises in the east and sets in the west. I'll navigate by the sun.

Then your heart sinks. Right now, the sun is hidden by a thick fog.

You're lost.

Try to find your way over to PAGE 63.

You paddle west for days. One afternoon you spot a ship a few miles away. But it steams off without spotting you. You slump over in your canoe in disappointment.

But you don't give up hope. You can't — your survival depends on it!

A few mornings later, a tiny island — an atoll — appears to the south. From this distance, you don't see any signs of life. Just palm trees swaying in the breeze.

Hmmm. The atoll may have food, you think. You're getting *really* sick of coconut milk. More important, you may find people.

On the other hand, you might find people who want to harm you.

Been there. Done that.

Should you take a chance and head for the atoll?

If you land on the atoll, go to PAGE 107.
If you bypass the atoll, go to PAGE 127.

The captain of the ship is a short, muscular man. He seems very friendly. He tells you that they are delivering cargo to a country in South America. He'll let you off at their first stop.

"Can you radio my parents?" you ask.

The captain clears his throat. "Ah, the radio isn't working. We're trying to fix it." He seems a little nervous.

Hold on, you think. What's the big deal about calling home?

A crewman leads you to your berth. "Just stay put," he orders. "Don't go wandering anywhere."

You sit on your bunk and read two-year-old magazines. At meals, you chow down with the crew. There are only five men on board. They don't talk to you. They just glare.

You try to be friendly. "So, guys," you start casually, "what kind of cargo are you carrying?"

A tough, greasy-haired sailor named Klink jumps up. "Why do you want to know?"

You shrug. "Just making conversation."

"Well, don't," another sailor warns you. "We like things nice and quiet."

You spend the rest of the meal studying your potato stew. When you return to your bunk, you realize: You still don't know what the ship's cargo is.

Go to PAGE 131.

124

Something bursts out of the water. Something huge.

You can't believe your eyes!

Behind you two giant lobsters rise out of the water. They must be six feet high. Their pincers are as big as jackhammers.

You tremble at the horrifying sight. Glenn whimpers beside you.

These aren't just giant lobsters. They're horrible mutants!

With human legs. Human eyes, noses, and mouths.

You want to flee, but your legs won't move.

"We were once like you," a lobster booms. "Passengers on a cruise. The Boss changed us."

The other lobster lunges toward you. "And now we want fresh flesh. Yours!"

Yikes! You've eaten lobster before — but you've never been eaten by a lobster!

You have to get away! But how? They're blocking the way you came in. Wait! There's a clear path to the hatch. Can you reach it before the lobsters catch you?

You glance up and spot a steam pipe on the ceiling. Hey! Don't restaurants steam lobsters? Maybe you could try that!

If you try to rush past the lobsters, go to PAGE 46.

If you try to break the steam pipe, go to PAGE 67.

You put down your paddle and stick your hand in the sea.

Brrr! The water is frigid. I wouldn't want to fall into *that*, you think. I'd be an ice cube in nothing flat.

Then a frightening thought worms its way into your mind. Could you have drifted off-course? You have a sickening feeling you sailed north instead of west.

If the compass is broken, you don't know which way to steer your little boat. While you sit in a daze, you hear a sound.

A-WHOOOOO! A-WHOOOOO!

It's a foghorn.

A ship must be nearby! Maybe everything will turn out okay!

You spot something white looming up ahead. Is it the ship? But you're sure the foghorn was coming from the opposite direction.

Which way should you go?

If you paddle toward the object, go to PAGE 73.

If you paddle toward the sound, go to PAGE 114.

126

Whoooaaa!

You fall into the water. But you're still holding on to the steam pipe. It breaks in two. Boiling-hot water pours out.

You jump out of the way. The chamber instantly fills with steam. The water starts getting hot.

The lobsters crawl away from the pipe.

While they scramble around to avoid the hot water, you run to the ladder. The water around you is beginning to bubble.

You reach the ladder and start to climb. Glenn is right behind you. From several feet up, you see the lobster creatures thrashing in the water. Their hard shells are turning bright red.

"What's happening to them?" Glenn asks.

"They're being steamed alive!" you answer. You can't stand to watch. You open the hatch and pop through.

And see something incredible.

View it on PAGE 79.

You avoid the atoll. Too risky. Instead, you continue west.

In the late afternoon you hear something like thunder. You glance back. A flash of light and a huge, mushroom-shaped cloud rise far in the distance.

Must be a terrible lightning storm over the atoll, you think. Good thing I didn't stop there.

You check the compass. For some reason, the needle is swinging around wildly. When it comes to rest, you use it to sail due west.

Over the next two weeks, the weather changes. It's getting cooler. You shudder. You wish you had a coat. Is it always this cold near Japan? you wonder.

Heavy fog rolls in. It's so thick, you can't see the front of the canoe.

You peer through it, confused. Where on earth are you?

See where you're headed on PAGE 125.

128

You're trapped in a net full of fish! It's being hauled by the boat that just passed.

With a lurch, the net rises out of the water. It settles on the back of the big boat. The net opens, spilling you and the wriggling fish down a chute. You all land on a conveyor belt.

Yikes! At the end of the belt is a fish-chopping machine!

"Help!" you shout. "I don't belong in here!"

But no one hears you.

I have to get off this belt! you realize. But a ton of fish sits on top of you. You get closer and closer to the whining blades of the chopper. Frantically you fling fish off your chest and legs.

With a loud grunt you push out from under the fish. You roll off the belt and drop to the floor.

Whew! You glance back at the machine. You escaped by mere inches. You quickly find a sailor. He's amazed to see you. He brings you to the captain.

He has bad news and worse news. He informs you that the trawler won't return to port for three months.

"I'll expect you to gut fish on this voyage," the captain orders. "Everyone pulls their weight on this ship. You're no exception."

Turn to PAGE 103.

You decide to paddle east — toward home. A strong ocean current makes your trip go faster. Awesome! This is the first good luck you've had since this horrible nightmare began.

One warm night you're sipping coconut milk and gazing at the night sky. At the horizon you spot a large red star moving quickly.

Wait a second, you think. Stars don't move that fast.

It could be a ship!

You paddle as fast as you can in the direction of the light. You were right. It *is* a ship!

You pull up close and yell as loudly as you can, "Help!"

No one answers. So you heave a coconut.

"Ouch!" someone cries. "Who threw that?"

A man in a dark cap looks over the side of the small ship. "Hey, there's someone in a canoe!"

A minute later you're climbing up a rope ladder. You're so happy, you babble thanks to everyone in sight.

The nightmare has officially ended!

Wake up on PAGE 123.

"Ye-owwch!" You glance down. A dart sticks out of your arm!

It was thrown by another competitor. "Oh, I'm terribly sorry," he apologizes. "I didn't see you there."

You yank out the dart and toss it to the floor. "How could you not see me?" you demand. You want to keep yelling at the guy. But you suddenly feel woozy.

You fall to your knees.

You stare at the dart that hit you. Green liquid seeps from the point.

"OHHHH!" you groan.

You realize that the tip of the dart was filled with some kind of poison. You'd be worried big-time — if you weren't losing consciousness.

"Gangway," the ship's doctor orders. "This person is ill."

The doctor kneels down beside you. "This is what you get for knowing too much," he whispers in your ear. "Need I explain more?"

"No, thanks," you gasp. "I got the point."

THE END

You're totally bored on board.

You have nothing to do. And no one to talk to. Everyone but the captain seems suspicious of you. What's up with that?

Two days later you wander downstairs to the cargo deck. Just to take a peek. But Klink spots you.

"Who gave you permission to snoop?" he snaps. "Beat it. Now!"

"Well, excuuuuuuse me," you grumble. Really ticked off, you turn around and climb back up to the main deck.

What's the big deal about the cargo? you wonder. What could it be? Bicycle wheels? Frisbees? Hamburger buns? Bean Babies?

Your curiosity gets the better of you. That night, you sneak down to the lower deck. You open the door to the cargo hold.

You turn on the light and step into the hold.

There are several crates inside marked FLOUR.

You pull back the top of a crate, breaking a wooden slate.

When you see what's inside, you gasp in surprise.

Find out what's so surprising on PAGE 52.

What you see is Mr. Smith — the guy who told you not to warn the captain about Bosco. Facing him is Mrs. Bass. Each holds a syringe.

"Move a muscle and I'll turn you into a flounder!" Mrs. Bass threatens Mr. Smith.

"Go ahead, make my day," Smith counters.

One of them must be the Boss! you realize.

Mrs. Bass shoots you a quick glance. "Help me," she cries. "He's the Boss. I came back to The Room to stop him. Now he's threatening to inject fish DNA into me. Save me!"

"She's lying," Smith shouts. "*She's* the Boss. My real name is Wolf Moldy. I'm a special agent of the Federal Fish and Game Department. I've been searching for the Boss for years. I finally tracked her to this ship. I've already called in reinforcements on my cell phone."

"He's insane," Mrs. Bass screams. "Pick up that fire extinguisher and shoot it at him, kids!"

"Don't listen to her," Smith orders. "Shoot the extinguisher at *her*! Hurry!"

You grab the fire extinguisher. Whoever you squirt will be blinded for a few seconds. Then you can overpower the Boss.

Whoever *that* is!

If you listen to Smith, go to PAGE 137.
If you listen to Mrs. Bass, go to PAGE 32.

Honesty is the best policy. So you admit you broke into the cargo hold.

Klink grins. "I knew it," he gloats.

The captain shakes his head. "Sorry. You know too much." He grabs you and hurls you over the side of the boat.

KERSPLOSH!

You swim to the surface. The ship is already out of reach. You're in deep water. And in deep trouble.

At least the water is warm, you think gratefully.

You wonder if you can tread water for several weeks.

Nope. You discover that twenty-five minutes is your limit.

Panic races through your bloodstream. Fear makes you flail around in the water.

"Ow!" Your hand strikes something hard.

You can't believe your eyes.

It's a tortoise. A GIANT tortoise.

The reptile is big enough to carry a passenger on its back. It's big enough to carry a family of four — plus luggage.

This is your ticket to safety!

You climb onto the tortoise's rough, wet back.

Float over to PAGE 84.

134

"You . . . are a HERO!" Smith drops the syringe and gives you a bear hug. You sigh in relief.

"You put the Boss out of business," Smith continues. "She won't be turning people into fish anymore."

You and Glenn high-five each other. You can't stop grinning.

"I'm a hero too," Glenn declares.

"Are you *fishing* for a compliment?" you snort.

"Duh," Glenn comments on your dumb joke.

"Speaking of which," Smith adds, "you kids care to join me for a fly-fishing trip next week?"

"We already caught the biggest fish ever," you answer, looking over at Mrs. Bass.

Smith steers Mrs. Bass to an elevator. It leads to the upper decks. The coast guard ship that Smith told you he alerted on his phone pulls alongside the *Finatic*.

They round up the Boss's thugs. Including Fisher. "Listen, guys," he bargains with the authorities. "I'll tell you everything Mrs. Bass did if you let me go."

Mrs. Bass goes ballistic. "You miserable little goldfish!" Before anyone can react, she breaks away and tears off Fisher's shirt.

For the big fin-ale, go to PAGE 69.

Honesty is the best policy. But not in this case, you decide.

"No way," you insist. "It wasn't me. I found a GOOSEBUMPS book under a sailor's cot. I couldn't put it down. I read it all night."

They nod. That story is certainly believable.

The captain lets you go. Klink grumbles. But there's nothing he can do.

The rest of the trip goes smoothly. The ship pulls into the harbor of a South American city.

Fifteen minutes later you and the entire crew are arrested for smuggling. You try to tell the police that you had nothing to do with it. But your Spanish isn't very good. And their English isn't too great either.

The good news is, the judge takes your age into account when he hands out the sentence:

You only have one life sentence to serve, instead of two!

THE END

136

You and Glenn are stunned by who you see. "What are you doing here, Mrs. Bass?" you ask.

She looks dazed. "I was kidnapped by the crew and taken down here. I managed to escape. But there is a cage full of passengers who didn't escape. You have to help them."

"Where are they?" Glenn wonders.

"Near the boiler room." She points to a dark passage. "I must warn passengers on the upper decks." She stumbles away.

You turn to Glenn. "We have to free those people."

He squints at Mrs. Bass as she races down the corridor. "She really knows her way around the ship," he notes.

As you walk toward the boiler, the air becomes hotter and hotter. Sweat drips off your face.

The corridor turns and widens. Built into the space is a large steel shark cage.

Mrs. Bass was right.

It's filled with people.

Go to PAGE 5.

Mrs. Bass has to be the Boss, you think. She had the chance to lock you in that cage. And how did she know her way around the boat so well? You spray her with the fire extinguisher.

"OOOW!" Mrs. Bass shrieks. "I can't see!"

The foam has temporarily blinded her. Glenn grabs her arm and knocks away the needle. It clatters to the floor.

Mrs. Bass drops to the floor in agony. You quickly find some electric cord and tie her arms behind her back.

"We beat Mrs. Bass!" you cheer. "The nightmare is finally over."

Or is it?

Smith turns to face you. He still grips the syringe tightly.

He advances toward you. The needle is pointing at your chest.

Wait a second. Is he the Boss after all?

The smile on your face fades.

You back off. You don't want to become some tuna or squid.

Smith's stubbly, sweaty face looks grim. He keeps coming. He mutters, "You . . . you . . ."

Back toward PAGE 134.

About R.L. Stine

R.L. Stine is the most popular author in America. He is the creator of the *Goosebumps*, *Give Yourself Goosebumps*, *Fear Street*, and *Ghosts of Fear Street* series, among other popular books. He has written over 250 scary novels for kids. Bob lives in New York City with his wife, Jane, teenage son, Matt, and dog, Nadine.